ENCORES
for a Dilettante

by

URSULE MOLINARO

FICTION COLLECTIVE NEW YORK

This publication is in part made possible with support from the National Endowment for the Arts in Washington, D.C.

This publication is in part made possible with support from the New York State Council on the Arts.

Grateful acknowledgment is also made for the support of Brooklyn College and Teachers & Writers Collaborative.

First Edition
Copyright © 1977 by Ursule Molinaro
All rights reserved
Library of Congress Catalogue No. 77-81003
ISBN: 0-914590-44-8 (cloth)
ISBN: 0-914590-45-6 (paper)
Published by FICTION COLLECTIVE
Distributed by George Braziller, Inc.
          One Park Avenue
          New York, New York 10016

FOR PETER SAINT-MU

By the same author

GREEN LIGHTS ARE BLUE
SOUNDS OF A DRUNKEN SUMMER
THE BORROWER
THE ZODIAC LOVERS
LIFE BY THE NUMBERS

Any resemblance with anyone that you know that I know is prototypical rather than personal.

The dilettante would like to prevail upon his readers: to grant him the exclusive right to put himself down.

He hopes that they will admire the candor of his various mirror images, not unlike he himself used to admire the candor of André Gide, for allowing readers of his *Journal* to play spider to his hypocrisies.

In other words: the dilettante begs for compassion. A luxury denied him by his sense of comparative superiority.

There is an instant of freedom immediately upon awakening in the morning   or whenever one wakes up   when life pauses. When the day ahead lies pristine & patternless like uncommitted soil ready for sowing. Wheat or weeds or flowers. Before remembrance of the night before   & of the string of days & nights before the night before   resurfaces, & recommits the present to the past, with its panorama of barbed-wired chicken coops.

On which the awakening limp-rising ego balloon impales itself.

>   C'est le supplice du pal
>   Qui commence si bien
>   & finit si mal.

>   It is the torture of impalement
>   That thrills to start
>   & ends in ailment.

Or, perhaps better:

>   It is the torture of impaling
>   That starts with thrills
>   & ends with wailing.

The balloon's flesh-colored shreds flap with fear. Afraid like a rabbit that runs from everything that it can't eat.

Flaking unfamiliar hotel room walls start showing through the madonna-blue screen of instant morning glories that can no longer conceal the slow-swaying bodies of 2 cats.

Sitting up in the unfamiliar hotel bed he tries to expand the waking instant of freedom. The moment of grace from continuity. Pretending not to remember why he is waking up in a hotel room. Why he is not waking up in his apartment, in the double bed, holding the freckled hand of his Irish concert-harpist wife Maureen. Who has rolled newspaper into her reddish hair   the reviews of her first official concert because she washed her hair before they went to bed the night before.

Or from a nap on his girlfriend Patricia's couch, holding the hand of his girlfriend Patricia. Holding *la patte de Pat* Pat's paw   whose French background has re-awakened his interest in French. Especially in medieval French poets, on whom Patricia is writing a thesis. Which he is helping her write; to help Patricia free herself from the trappings of her heritage.

He tries   but fails   to convince himself that he has awakened in a hotel room in an unfamiliar city. On a cross-country concert tour. After an evening of standing ovations.

Which coincided happily with the eve of his 45th birthday.

He tries to repel the bottle of champagne which resurfaces with the thought of his birthday.

He had bought it on his way home from dinner with

Patricia. Putting P. into a cab rather than walking her home & staying for a round of night-cap loving on her couch. He had wanted to make sure he arrived at his house well before midnight, in plenty of time for the traditional midnight toast he & his freckle-faced Irish concert-harpist wife Maureen had grown fond of drinking   with champagne   on the eve of their birthdays.

& for the last 2 years also on the birthdays of their red cat Leon Katz, the one of their 2 cats whose birthday they knew because he had been born in the apartment 3 years ago.

He had taught Leon Katz to ride around the apartment on his shoulders. & to transfer from his shoulders onto his wife's invitingly stooped back. To make sure his wife didn't feel excluded from his intimacy with the cat.

The bottle must still be standing wherever he had set it down.

On the radiator beside the entrance, when he reached for the light switch: he remembers only too well. Would prefer not to remember. His disconcertion, stepping into a dark apartment. The sensation of clammy cat fur brushing against his face.

Perhaps the bottle has exploded from the heat. The mushroom-shaped cork straining in the wires, tearing itself free. Shattering the glass of the not-quite-finished portrait of Catherine   long for Cat   their first; mother of Leon Katz. Which he had started to paint 8 or 9 years ago. In the studio of his girlfriend Leonora. Who painted. & sewed for a living.

He had painted the cat after a photograph he had taken of Catherine, as a surprise for his wife, while Leonora painted him painting the cat. For which he had commissioned Leonora, to help her gain confidence in her talent. To make her stop sewing, & paint full time.

& to get over her irrational fear of cats.

His wife had hung the not-quite-finished painting on the

wall across from the entrance, where he could not not see it when he came home.
Even last night he'd been aware of it.

He must go back to the apartment. But not just yet. He has until noon to check out of the hotel room.

In which he has just awakened from a nightmare that has absolutely no relation to the successful reality of his life: he briefs himself: He'd love to know how C. G. Jung would interpret his unrelated nightmare.
He is in an unfamiliar city (remember!) in which he gave a concert & received standing ovations the night before.
Any moment, the local reporters plus a handful of foreign correspondents with a particularly keen flair for what is happening anywhere in the music world; even in this unfamiliar, as yet nameless city will come pouring through the door of his modest hotel room, armed with notebooks & tape recorders, & other implements of professional indiscretion. & corner him still in bed; sitting cross-legged on the pillow, in shirt & underpants (in which he slept) & subject him to an interview.
That will also be televised.
& he prays that the as yet nameless lady pianist Semantha, maybe who accompanied him last night, before, during & after ovations; all the way into his modest single hotel bed, for a champagne-less precelebration of his 45th birthday (Semantha refuses to believe that he is 45!) will linger in the bathroom until the reporters have finished their job, & left.
(The bathroom is way down the hall. Up to last night he didn't have the bread for a private bath, on concert tours.)
Not because he wishes to exclude Semantha from sudden recognition, from the music world's finally waking up to the fact that he has talent. Far from it. She deserves her share, as his accompanist. But because he doesn't want any trace of her

presence in his hotel bed to leak into the papers. & onto the TV screens all over the country. & upset his girlfriend Patricia. Who is too recent in his life to be accustomed to the fact that he likes women.

Who is still reluctantly becoming accustomed to the fact that he has a wife. Maureen. Who has reddish hair. & freckles all the way down into her cleavage. & a slightly blueing tooth on the upper left side of her mouth, which shows when she smiles. An Irish concert-harpist, to whose first official concert he had taken P., 10 days ago. & who has become fully accustomed. & is too absorbed in her harp to give the fact that he likes women much thought. He had thought.

Perhaps his wife was practicing her harp at this very moment. Wherever she was, at this very moment.

She'd be practicing in the hotel room, if she'd come with him on the concert tour. If he'd gone on a consort-concert tour.

She'd be sitting on the only chair in front of the closet, with gently inclined bust still in her nightgown stroking her harp.

& if anybody banged on the walls, or the manager telephoned & complained about neighbors complaining, she'd point out that a professional concert-harpist was entitled to as much professional noise as the 5 yellow-helmeted men who have been tearing up the sidewalk outside the hotel entrance under the dust-curtained window since the blueing hours of dawn.

& if the manager argued over the telephone that yellow-helmeted professional noise had a higher earning average than the rainbow sounds of stretched cat gut, & therefore unlike the latter deserved to be respected & listened to, she'd quote Tagore at him: "God respects me when I work, but He loves me when I sing." & the manager would be convinced, & hang up.

Although: Love is *his* type of argument, not his Irish concert-harpist wife's. Who rarely uses the word. & tells him that he doesn't know what he's talking about when *he* uses it.

A professor of English literature should pay closer attention to the meaning of the words he uses: she says to him. & not confuse lust with love. Which is unfamiliar ground for a professional seducer.

'If you were a professional *violinist,* you'd be out of bed & practicing. & the rest of your life would fall into place': she says, straightening her bust on the only hotel chair in front of the closet. Her nipples are pointing through the nightgown.

'What do you mean, you don't have your instrument with you? A professional seducer goes nowhere without his instrument.'

She is laughing at him. At the way he is sitting, cross-legged on the pillow, in his shirt & underpants. Making a pedestal for his stomach. Which is resting on his knees.

'Is he perhaps onto something new?' she inquires. 'Is he already through with that tall French chick what's-her-name Patricia? & is his new girlfriend a hatha yoga teacher by any chance?'

A welcome change of interests, in her opinion. Not that she has anything against tall French chicks. Or chubby medieval poets. Nor does she believe in hatha yoga just for the sake of exercise. Still, sitting in the lotus position might surreptitiously open a morning-glory in his head.

She is teasing him. About his ready change of interests. Which he willingly admits often coincides with a change of girlfriends. He is not ashamed of his versatility. Which will add depth to his writing, when he gets around to writing, after he finishes taking notes on life.

It is keeping his mind flexible. His face looking younger than his age.

'Like a green apple that would rather rot than ripen,' laughs his wife. Who has never been a country girl. Her knowledge of apples is limited to the delicatessen. 'He's right to try to preserve himself; he's a slow learner.'

She can't stop teasing him about his preoccupation with the way he looks. Youthful. Hip. He defies anybody to guess what he does for a living.

She admires that, actually. She doesn't want to be the wife of a parchment-lipped professor of Eng. Lit. Who spends every class-free hour crouched inside a cobweb of academic considerations & reconsiderations, writing away the life he doesn't dare live.

About which he knows little. Knows only what he has read in books. By other professors. Whom he feels compelled to imitate. & to outdo. Not because he has something to say & feels the urge to say it. But because the faculty expects him to publish.

She shakes her reddish hair. & smiles one of her freckled blueing smiles. Of course she doesn't.

She is quoting something from *Two or Three Graces,* by Aldous Huxley. Which she teasingly calls: Two or Three *Dis*graces.

She loves him the way he is. Chubby & playful. She's a little proud of being the only wife in his harem.

He'd always thought.

His mind takes a side trip. Deliberately. To get off the subject of his wife. (Whom he will divorce, if that's what she wants. Let her find out what her talent is worth without a husband to support her.) He gives himself a birthday party. For his 35th birthday rather than for the 45th. Which is today.

If he were famous   a famous painter; a much published writer; the recently interviewed violinist in the modest hotel room in the unfamiliar nameless city   he'd be considered young no matter what his age, considering his timeless achievements. Unlike the 45-year-old Who-Are-You who has just awakened in the same hotel room in an all too familiar city & pretends to be 35   a 35 he never was   in an effort to convince himself that the present has no reason to accept its inheritance from the past. That a mistake is a mistake only if we insist . . . While listening to cavities being drilled into the sidewalk outside the hotel entrance.

He can also not check out at noon. & spend a second night in this shabby-walled noisy no-man's land.

He is inviting all his former girlfriends to his 35th-birthday banquet. Every girl or woman he remembers going to bed with since highschool. All the way down the line to his current girlfriend Patricia.

He seats them in chronological order from left to right around a 100-foot-long dining table in a hotel ballroom he rents for the occasion. The first one   his baby sister's German babysitter, whose name was 'Head', short for Hedwig   on his right.

'Head' has cut the arm-thick shiny red braid she used to wear half-down her back. By which he'd pulled her down on the floor beside the crib   on top of him   the first time they made love   the first time he made love all the way   while his baby sister cried herself blue in the face.

Developing the powerful lungs with which she belted her way to fame, as a teenage rock singer.

His sister used to lock herself into the bathroom, between the ages of 12 & 14, turn all 4 faucets on full force, & scream her hatred of the world against the roar of running water. For hours. Instead of doing her homework. Getting lower &

lower grades. Getting fatter & fatter. Driving their beautiful mother to the brink of a nervous breakdown.

They had shipped her off to a boarding school, finally. Which they could ill afford, on their father's hick-town highschool teaching salary. It had deprived him of the motorcycle he'd been promised for a BA *summa cum laude*. Instead of the second-hand bicycle his father bought him.

His sister had sent him a Harley-Davidson later from England; together with a sable evening stole for their beautiful mother after she'd been 'discovered', at the boarding school. & dropped out. & become a fat teenage idol, at 16. Or maybe at 17. When he & his beautiful mother couldn't walk into a music store without his sister's fat pig-eyed face glinting at them from a stack of record albums. Or from a poster.

& then his sister had suddenly disappeared. Shortly after she'd turned 20. When she'd gone to a retreat, or something, & had lost 100 lbs. Before she entered the Irish nunnery in which she's been living ever since.

Which she has made famous & rich with her singing. Only love songs now. About the everlasting love of God. & of Jesus. & of the Immaculate Mother. Which she sings only on Christmas & Easter & Pentecost.

His sister has turned down his cabled invitation to sing at his birthday banquet. Of which she isn't sure she approves. At which she'd only feel misplaced. She can't recall any incestuous feelings between them.

She does, however, recall the German babysitter's braid.

& the German babysitter's brother. Who she recalls had stolen the motorcycle she sent him. A couple of days after it arrived. Before he'd had a chance to ride it. Why had he never called the police? & tried to get it back? she'd like to know. He hadn't been afraid to ride it, had he?

She's also congratulating him. On his marriage rather than his 35th birthday. (Which she thought he had celebrated 10 years ago.) She somehow hadn't expected him to get married.

He has seated his freckle-faced Irish concert-harpist wife Maureen at the other small end of the table, across from him. They're toasting each other across 100 feet of immaculate damask blank.

Behind each plate he has placed a trinket   or a flower   that sums up the relationship he's had with each. A tortoise-shell comb for 'Head'. A ram's head ring for Ilona.

They arrive. But not in chronological order. He should have staggered the arrival time at 10-minute intervals when he wrote out the invitations.

A few invitations are returned: Addressee unknown.

2 or 3 don't come. But call. & express the desire to see him again   alone   at some other time & place.

2 or 3 don't come. & don't call.

Some are chronic late-comers. & haven't changed; in that respect.

All have aged considerably. Considerably more than he has aged, by comparison. Considering that he's 35. He could easily pass for a chubby 28, 29. It jeopardizes his authority with his students, sometimes.

Numbers 2 through 10 look positively matronly. After #10 they fall into a younger age bracket, with 2 or 3 exceptions. Female students have a tendency to fall in love with their Eng. Lit. profs.

Who indulge them. It keeps their language up to date.

They've grown taller, too. Patricia is a regular amazon, in spite of her French background.

They sit. Play with their napkins. Sip at their cocktails. Nibble on a strip of carrot. Eyeing each other. Each speculating about his relationship with the others. Especially with the one to their right. Who was the one right after.

#5 can't see what he saw in #6. What did #6 have then

that #5 was then lacking? Was #9 perhaps a return to something he had started with #7? Or way before #7? With #4 perhaps?

His interest in painting, for instance, did it start before or after #4?

Way after #4, actually. #4 had been his mother's psychiatrist. Dr. Catherine Spoon. Who introduced him to a new exciting world of Orgon boxes & Viennese mythology & Chinese oracles.

& Bruno Bettelheim. He had considered teaching autistic children for a while.

There had been a rather rapid succession of girlfriends, after #4. After several years of Dr. Spoon's psycho-analytical encouragement to self-express. A bi-monthly to quarterly turnover, between numbers 5 through 12.

His interest in painting began with Leonora. #13. His first girlfriend after his marriage. After he'd been married for some 2 to 3 years. & ended with Leonora, when he realized his helplessness in front of the live cat Leonora had coaxed up to her studio, one afternoon. To get him off copying a cat after a photograph.

Leonora has probably stopped painting altogether. & has been sewing full time, since they broke up.

He had sacrificed Leonora to save his marriage. To give his freckle-faced rusty-haired Irish harpist-wife more time to grow accustomed to the fact that he likes women.

Which detracted in no way from his love for her: he had assured his wife, when she found out about the existence of Leonora in his life.

From him. When he told his wife about the existence of Leonora in his life. To be able to stop lying about additional curricula. He has a horror of sneaking around.

Leonora's existence wasn't taking anything away from their love: he had reassured his wife. On the contrary. He was brimming over with love, since their marriage. He had love enough inside him for the entire universe. His wife had nothing to worry about. She was the only woman he wanted to live with.

Which was not what was worrying his wife. Security was not foremost on her mind. Nor was she jealous. But she was unwilling to be used as the headquarters for his promiscuity.

Which was *not* the path toward universal love: *she* had assured *him*. Fidelity was that path, paradoxical though that might sound to him. Unhip though that might sound to him. It was only through loving *one* person completely that one learned to love the rest of humanity.

Not physically, obviously. Making love to anyone but the person one loved was inconceivable to her. If one really loved that one person.

He shouldn't have married   at least he shouldn't have married her   if he has no talent for fidelity.

Why *had* he married her? Rather than one of the others? She'd have gone to bed with him a couple of times, if that was all he'd wanted from her. If she had realized that he kept confusing his heart with his hard-ons.

Marriage was another matter.

To her it was a sacred hermetic union. The alchemical blender which fused skin & soul & transformed lust into love.

Which couldn't last unless it was allowed to grow. & how could it grow, if it was constantly exposed to outside elements? A foetus died when air was introduced into the womb.

His famous autobiography, his novels, & brilliant essays, & revolutionizing textbooks would never get written as long as he kept talking them away. To overwhelm prospective girlfriends with his brilliance. Throwing pearls before chicks.

Did he know that according to Jean Giraudoux Sodom & Gomorrha might have been saved if the angels had been able to find a single united couple in either of the 2 wicked cities?

Which was more the type of quiz question he likes to pop at his students. At Patricia, occasionally. His wife is not particularly literary-minded. She's a harpist. Which may align her with the angels, but not with Jean Giraudoux who was not particularly famous for conjugal fidelity.
Few famous men were model husbands.

She had picked up their cat & her harp & walked out.

He couldn't find her when he walked out after her, a few minutes later. After he got over his astonished annoyance.
He had spent 3 days looking for her. Calling the school to say that he was sick. That he was still sick   that he had a virus   a stomach virus that was keeping him trapped in the bathroom for 3 consecutive days   while he'd combed the streets.

He must call the school before noon.

Finally he had found her. Shortly before midnight, midtown, in a French restaurant. In an unfamiliar evening gown. Sitting under a potted palm with gently inclined grey-satin bust, stroking her harp for the diners better to dine by.
For over a month he had eaten better French dinners which he could ill afford to eat every night for over a month   (He'd gained 15 lbs.)   & had dropped Leonora   & collected his not-quite-finished portrait of their cat Cat-herine from Leonora's studio as proof that he was not going back to Leonora's studio   & begun to take violin lessons, as proof that he was interested in his wife's interests   until she had finally let herself be persuaded to come home.

She'd been different, after she came home.

She began to practice her harp much more than before. Most of the day. Even on weekends.

She was no longer standing in the door of their apartment with cat-Catherine in her arms & a Bourbon in her hand for him   like a red-light-district madonna, when he came home from school.

He'd find her in the bedroom, bent over her harp. Nodding a distracted freckle-smile in his direction as he entered. & took his violin from its coffin. & went to the living room to practice for a couple of interminable hours, to prove to her that he was keeping his word.

She'd still be practicing when he finished practicing. & poured himself a drink. & went to the kitchen, finally, to fry a couple of hamburgers for both of them.

Perhaps she practiced most of the day only on weekends. & did nothing during the day the rest of the week. Just sat around, cross-legged on the living room rug. & played with the cats. Or hypnotized her freckles away in the bathroom mirror. & began practicing only shortly before he came home.

Later again, since she paid no attention to him when he was at home. & wasn't cooking any dinners.

He stopped practicing the violin   on which he wasn't making much progress; unlike his wife who was making noticeable progress on her harp   & started eating dinner out, after he met Ilona. His Greek girlfriend. #14. Who was an actress. & answered telephones for a living. & tried to make him interested in Women's Lib. & in the Aquarian age.

Who revived his interest in Greek mythology & classical Greek drama. He had thought of majoring in ancient history, at one point, when he was still in highschool.

He started going to Ilona's rehearsals. & watched. & waited for the director to finish giving notes, to have a drink with Ilona. & encourage her to drop her job with the answering service & act full time. To show herself worthy of her classical Greek heritage.

His wife is still practicing her harp when he comes home. At 11:30 p.m. She smiles a freckled blueing smile & reluctantly accepts his invitation to go with him to watch Ilona rehearse Medea.

They sit side by side in the cold empty theatre. They wait for the director to finish giving notes. They have drinks with Ilona & discuss the play.

Ilona has many unorthodox ideas on the subject of Medea. Which she cannot share with her director. Who thinks actors & especially actresses should act, not think. Who thinks he's got a hot-line to Euripides' brain.

He'd replace Ilona, if she told him that she thinks the Golden Fleece stands for the dying Arien age. At the point of transition into the Piscean age.

For which Ilona has no use. Because of what it did to women. Watering the strong-minded ardently equal amazon down to a resigned mother figure. With the Madonna as the compromise between goddess & mother.

Medea is the last true Arien-age woman. The last of a long line of white goddesses, white witches & healers who related to their contemporaries, not to their children. Whom they raised to stand on their own 2 feet. Not as surrogate husbands, & old-age companions.

That's why Medea kills her children when Jason leaves her. Not because she's jealous of an insipid little crown princess who'll always be her daddy's daughter. Who'll never grow into a proudly mature woman. But to protest against being turned into a man-less mother figure, into the new Piscean-age woman, by a new Piscean-age opportunist. A middle-aging adolescent. Who is as ruthless as he is sentimental. Who is trying to ride the cusp between 2 ages. & thinks the present can escape paying its dues to the past.

Jason never loved   only used   Medea. His love is

reserved for his buddies. & for his sons. Women count only in bed. & even there they're penalized. They're made into mothers.

Ilona hates Jason. More than Medea hated Jason, after the betrayal. Ilona has no use for married men who run around. If his wife didn't happen to be present she'd probably be telling him again what a son of a pig she thinks he is for wanting to make love to her.

Which is what she told him after he told her that he was married, after he made love to her for the first time. Because he has a horror of lying.

Ilona has no use for liars either. She shares the low opinion liars must have of themselves, or else they wouldn't bother lying. They're liveried souls, suspended between double standards.

Why didn't he tell her that he was married *before* he made love to her? Before he made her betray her sexual solidarity. 'The other woman in his life . . . told him: go home & scratch your wife . . .' she told him. Quoting a Burma-shave road ad.

Sleeping with a married man was always an emotional lie, even if it was done semi-overtly, with the wife turning a condoning back. To get the liar off her back, most likely. Or because she was still blind-folded, & hadn't yet emerged from the myth that men are naturally biologically polygamous. Hogamus/higamus. Whereas women were   higamus/hogamus
   naturally biologically monogamous.

'If male supremacy sprouts on your chin, go shave it off, don't rub it in:' she said to him. Ilona had at one point tried to sell Burma-shave jingles. Which had, however, been rejected. For obvious pig reasons.

He shouldn't have married, if he has no talent for fidelity: Ilona informed him. In the words of his wife. Not because Ilona considered marriage a sacred hermetic union, but because 'he has made his bed, & should lie in it!'

He'd enjoy lying in it & nowhere else if he weren't the typical Piscean-age pig who married the mother of his children, & went elsewhere for his pleasures.

The fact that he has no children that his wife is a concert-harpist who has no time to have children; that they have 2 cats instead of children makes no difference to Ilona.

Maybe he's sterile, & doesn't know it.

Knows it subconsciously, probably. That's why he felt he needed the social reassurance of marriage.

Which is a con game. Played by paternalistic Piscean-age pigs who have restricted women to 2 roles: mother & whore. Who have made cunts out of women by sanctifying the breeding process. After prudently removing the pleasure aspect from conception by putting emphasis on immaculacy.

Pleasure makes equals. Duty distinguishes between master & slave.

Paternalistic Piscean-age pigs think a woman who expects pleasure in bed is a whore. (She, Ilona, is not a whore; if that's what *he* thinks.) Regardless of the blatant fact that a whore does not expect pleasure from a client, merely money.

Ilona is counting on the Aquarian age to get her equality back. Not the ardent pleasure-for-pleasure equality of Medea's Arien age, but a brother-sister equality, with playfully incestuous overtones.

& shared child care. Which will automatically curtail overpopulation.

Besides, there would be an Aquarian-age population-control law, penalizing couples who produced more than one child. Even if the couples changed partners. Having another 'first' with a new partner would be illegal. Second, third, etc., offenders would be apprehended as perpetrators of genocide. Causing more than one life would become as serious a crime as murder . . .

He is beginning to suspect that Ilona is maybe a Lesbian. In spite of her more than adequate performance in bed, that first time, before he told her that he was married.

Of course she may have faked it. She is after all an actress.

Perhaps rehearsing Medea four times a week has leaked into her off-stage personality. & all men have become Jason to her.

For whatever reason his wife also hates Jason. & therefore does not hate Ilona. (Perhaps she also suspects Ilona of being a Lesbian? Maybe?)

Watching Medea has purged her of a need for private drama. She's had a couple of drinks. She's over hating his girlfriends. Who are in the plural. Whereas she is unique in his life. His only wife. She knows he doesn't want to live with anyone else. Jealousy is so unhip. An antiquated possessive Piscean-age emotion.

She has come around to his views on marriage. & is enjoying the modern freedom it affords both partners, on the warm basis of unpossessive mutual love & trust. He thinks. They can afford to be totally frank with each other.

He thinks.

He makes a point of introducing his new girlfriends to his wife. Right at the beginning, after he's gone to bed with them once or twice. To set her mind at ease by allowing her to feel superior.

('I despise myself when I look at myself. But I'm filled with admiration when I compare myself,' his Leo-mother used to say. To his ceaselessly admiring Pisces father.)

& to forestall any confusion on the part of his girlfriends, as to his ultimate intentions.

They joke about how uptight some of these liberated girls are when he introduces them to 'his wife'. About the tight-laced Victorian expectations some of them wear under their emancipated serapes, their loose capes; in their determined amazon boots.

All his girlfriends know he loves & respects his wife very much.

Patricia had been sweet & respectful, the first time she met his wife.

Who realizes that she's being respected.

It makes her feel as though she were his mother. Which is probably what he married her for. What he married for. To have a mother all to himself. Without any competition from daddy. A hip mother to whom he brings his girlfriends home for approval.

His girlfriends don't need her approval. Not any more than they need his help, if they really are the actresses or painters or poets he introduces them as being. If they're not just playing at being actresses or painters or poets the way he's playing at helping them fulfill themselves. In the seduction game he's playing with them. & they with him. Each smiling at how he/she is duping the other. All duping themselves all the while.

All condescendingly commiserating with 'the wife'. The biggest dupe of them all. His captive soledad mother whom he sporadically gratifies with a bout of incest. For which the dumb lonely bitch is grateful. A hard man is good to find.

Especially for a married woman. Whom most men consider private property, with unliberated dyed-in-the-wool male solidarity. & they'd rather not trespass, lest it get them 'in trouble with the man'. Lest they get stuck with supporting the married woman. Who has become accustomed to being supported, obviously. Whom the husband is trying to dump, obviously. Or else he wouldn't be looking the other way. She can't be much good if she's playing around . . .

His wife is *not* enjoying the freedom of their modern marriage. Freedom from what? she asks. From fidelity?

Why should running around, trying to pick up me-too affairs mean freedom to her, just because *he* is running around? Painting me-too pictures. Making me-too music. Enslaving himself in fulfilled banality.

Can he think of anything more banal than middle-aging promiscuity? She'd rather practice her harp . . .

She'd better. She may not have the opportunity much longer, after he divorces her. Without a cent of alimony, courtesy of Women's Lib. Let her establish her own credit. With Con Ed & Bell Tel. Let her open her own charge accounts. He can be liberated too.

His 35th birthday dinner is a great success.

The alcoholically inclined drink exuberantly of the wine. Which is French. & excellent. His wife is toasting him for the 13th time.

The food-oriented have several helpings of the Boeuf Wellington. Which is also excellent. Cooked by his current girlfriend Patricia.   (Who can't cook. Whom he hadn't met when he was 35. Who was 9 when he was 35.)   #23. Who feels superior to all the other girls or women around the table. Who form the ladder on which she has climbed to the seat on his left. But feels inferior to his wife   whom she has met; twice   for not being his wife. For not sitting 100 feet across/away from him.

He realizes with a shock that he has forgotten to invite Carey. His selfish Giant. The fattest girlfriend he's had. A 5′2″ cube. With delicate wrists & ankles. & beautifully shaped gigantic legs. & glowing skin. A monument encased in satin. Who never passed unnoticed. Who preferred to die young rather than diet, & live longer as an average little woman of 5′2″ for whom only average men might turn around.

How could he have forgotten Carey. He owes her most of his knowledge of food & wines.

She used to make him feel like a Turkish potentate, when

they walked into a restaurant. Where she always picked up the tab. Which was always large.

& she always checked out the chair before she sat down. Because she had once sat down on her nephew's Christmas puppy.

Suddenly, #13   Leonora   lays down her napkin, pushes back her chair, & walks out.

She's still resentful because he dropped her to save his marriage before they'd had enough of each other. Besides, she is frustrated because she has stopped painting & is sewing full time, to make a living.

#10 walks out after her. She's a Leo, like his mother. Who had also run from competition.

(To the wilds of Pennsylvania. Where she could play frog-princess in a small pond. & sing Brahms at local charity bashes. & bring tears to the eyes of the local listeners who hadn't realized that their beautiful mysterious neighbor had such a beautiful voice. Which deserved to be heard in big concert halls in big cities.

Unlike the undeserving voice of the beautiful mysterious neighbor's not-at-all-beautiful fat teenage daughter. What a tragedy for a beautiful woman to have such an ungracious daughter . . .)

To forestall further defections he stands up & suggests that they dance. Although Patricia's cherry jubilee   a most appropriate dessert for the occasion   has not yet been served.

To avoid jealousies he will dance with each one in chronological order. To the special song that used to be 'their' song while they were lovers. He has kept the records. An impressive stack. Some are in foreign languages. German. Greek. French.

He has placed them on the record player in chronological order. #13 is missing. Leonora broke their song when he broke with her to save his marriage. & stamped her foot on it. & used the broken pieces in a collage.

He holds out his arms to #1.

They dance. The others sit & watch. He bows. Holds out his arms to #2. They dance. The others sit and watch. He bows. Holds out his arms to #3.

He hasn't finished the languid tango he is dancing with #4   Dr. Catherine Spoon; who looks older & less beautiful than his mother looked on her deathbed   when the others stop watching. & push back their chairs. & rise.

They seem taller than he remembers them. Even the more recent younger taller ones.

They're stepping out of their skirts; their pants.

Stiff & tall they advance toward the dance floor, naked from the waist down, except for their boots.

Dr. Spoon disengages herself from his arms & withdraws into the circle that has formed around him. That is dancing around him. That spins him to his knees.

Amazon boots are trampling on his legs. A solitary high heel impales his left thigh. He shields his skull with his hands, anticipating the kick of death.

Through a forest of shapely legs   he's always had a thing about legs   he can see the singing Irish face of his concert-harpist wife Maureen. Still sitting at her small end of the deserted table. A freckled modern-dress Medea/Judith Anderson/Maria Callas. Ilona. Beating out the rhythm of the still spinning song with the handle of her knife.

Substituting her own words for the lyrics of the song:

'His path to universal love
is lined with milestoned sex.

A lonely hedge of stony chicks
on which he lifts his dogged legs.

A whirlpool of vacuity
is spinning in his head.

Professional promiscuity
is keeping him in bed.'

Meanwhile, back at the French restaurant, the dilettante's widow is sitting under a potted plastic palm with gently mourning grey-satin bust, stroking her harp for midtown diners better to dine by.

She has not gone back to the French restaurant to play digestive songs to an applause of forks & knives. She is playing subversive lullabies to the mad children at Bellevue. Who are clapping with their wooden spoons.
    Into each of which Leonora has painted a wide-open blue eye.

Wide-eyed blue-eyed Leonora had spent time at Bellevue, after she tried to hang herself from her skylight. On his 36th birthday, a couple of months after they broke up.
    Leonora had called his house while he was at school. Knowing that he was at school. & had told his wife to tell him that 'Leonora was hanging herself'. With the leather tie she had sewn for him for his 36th birthday. Leonora would be dead by the time he came home from school. & would haunt him & his wife for the rest of their marriage. Every time they'd reach out to make love they'd feel the ghost of Leonora lying between them . . .   Confident that his wife would call him at the school the instant she hung up. & that he   & not 2 ambulance attendants   would come flying to her house, up the 5 flights of stairs, & catch her just as she was about to kick her sewing machine out from under her.
    She must have waited for close to an hour, standing on her sewing machine with his leather birthday tie around her neck.

He would have broken with her then, if he hadn't broken with her before. His mother's life has made him wary of dramatic women. Actresses should stick to the stage.

Leonora   he remembers   had been afraid of cats.

His wife has moved his 35th-birthday banquet to the terminal ward at Bellevue. All his former girlfriends   including Patricia   followed in single file when she led the way, playing her harp.

They are seated around the operating table   in blatant disregard of chronological order   & are holding a goldfish-swallowing contest, umpired by Dr. Cat-herine Spoon. Who is lecturing them on the importance of getting even with Ernest.

Having been lovers is a natural reason for becoming enemies: she tells them. The goldfish stands for their ex-lover. They must swallow it in order to get even. With all men, even with their inimitable daddies, their fixated sons.

Perhaps he has made more enemies than he thought. Of most of the girls &/or women with whom he'd thought he had parted the best of friends, after he stopped going to bed with them.

Most of whom had also been ready to stop, but hadn't said so first.

Perhaps Ilona has organized all her successors   with the exception of Patricia   to avenge the wife of a man-who-ran-around. In the name of liberty & equality. Even though Ilona had stopped going to bed with *him,* after that first & only time. When he had been far from ready to stop going to bed with her. Ilona probably considered running around a prerogative of liberating Aquarian-age women. Whose imagination   like that of most revolutionaries   probably didn't reach beyond a reversal of roles.

Perhaps Ilona had updated Euripides & staged a Women's Lib. adaptation of Medea in the apartment, on the eve of his

45th birthday. With the active collaboration of his freckle-faced red-haired Irish concert-harpist wife. Who hates him more than she loved their cats.

He must call the school & supply a satisfactory explanation for his absence. A combination of fiction & facts. Of the little he knows of the facts:
His apartment was broken into. & he broke his right arm struggling with 2 junkies whom he had surprised in the act of executing his 2 cats. As a revenge, because they had found nothing worthwhile in the apartment of a notoriously underpaid professor of English literature.
He has also broken his left ankle & won't be able to run around for a while. Walk or stand around while teaching, that is. He's been on the phone all morning, trying to rent a wheelchair.

(Trade-named: SPRITE.
Which will furnish the theme for his next mid-term paper. On the cynicism of advertising that stops at nothing to hook the public mind.
That gives P.O. Box #20-20 as the mailing address for tax-deductible donations to the blind . . .
It should wake up his English majors who are hoping to become Mad. Ave. Shakespeares rather than writing professors or teaching writers.)

He can't expect the faculty to lavish limitless sympathy upon a teacher with a broken arm who is mourning the death of cats.
Which are associated with the female weaker element. & therefore with deceit, the weapon of the weak.
He'd be better off mourning a dead dog. Or better still a horse. Especially if the horse had been a working horse whose

death might be respectably mourned as a financial loss.

Why is he mourning the death of animals? Has he no children, at age 45? His son might be just old enough to die in Vietnam. Is his wife barren? Or is he perhaps sterile? & is that why he's been sleeping around? A closet queen, maybe? Who'd rather swish than fight? With the 2 vindictive junkies of his imaginary alibi.

Has he been sleeping with women in order to punish them? & himself as well, since no private person can punish another with impunity. Inflicting the torture of impaling upon any halfway willing girl or woman. & has he now reached the wailing stage of selfpity, staying in bed mourning his 45th birthday, rather than the loss of his wife.
Whom he has denied the fulfillment of motherhood. Whom the 2 imaginary junkies might very well have executed also, when they found nothing worthwhile in the apartment.
Where she may be lying   dead   on the bed. With a stab wound in her heart. A crumple of stiffening flesh at the bottom of the closet into which the 2 junkies stuffed her after they strangled her after they raped her.
Is his sense of marriage less developed than that of the royal peacocks of Kensington that cried for months after foxes ate all the peahens while the males took refuge in the trees?

He *is* mourning the loss of his wife. But his wife's not dead. She's gone. She has walked out on him again. For the second time. With her harp.   —He'd always thought husbands walked out on wives, not wives on husbands . . . & this time she's taken her clothes   he checked both closets   but no cat.
The man she walked out with is terrified of cats. Because he'd been scratched by a kitten once, when he was a boy of

5   or maybe only 3   when a playful uncle at the seashore had placed the kitten on top of his head, to amuse the boy's mother.

The former boy is the pianist who accompanied his wife 10 days ago, when she gave her first official concert. When she became a recognized concert-harpist.

He had gone to her concert, 10 days ago. & he'd taken Patricia along, to make sure his wife would be applauded by at least 2 persons in the audience. He had shouted: "Bravo!" & Patricia had shouted: "Brava!", because P. knows not only French, but also Italian. Together they had set off a storm of applause   ovations   shouts for encores.

Which his freckle-flushed wife had neither expected nor wished him to do. With or without the cooperation of his large polyglot girlfriend.

It has freaked her out. She has gone stark raving mad with unexpected recognition. & is killing everything she's loved in the past to clear her path to success. To be free to go on to bitter beggar things.

He was probably wise not to have slept in the apartment last night, if she still loves him, after Leonora.

& he's lucky that she doesn't know that he's staying at the hotel. In room 401.

She probably assumes that he is staying at some hotel. If the suddenly recognized concert-harpist bothers assuming anything about the husband she has deserted. His staying at a hotel had been part of their arrangement, after he began introducing his girlfriends to her, after Leonora. He is no upholder of double standards. No Turkish potentate who has an adulterous woman tied naked into a sack, together with a living cat. & watches the sack drown while he distractedly fingers the bosom of another woman. Any time his wife wanted to have someone   a boyfriend   stay overnight, he was willing to go & spend that night at a hotel: he had promised her. He realized that most women preferred to make love at home. In familiar surroundings . . .

It had been a genuine promise. Which he had meant to keep. He would have gone to a hotel, rather than call his current girlfriend   Patricia   to ask if he might spend the night at her place, while his wife . . . But there had been no man staying over in the dark apartment. & no wife. Only 2 dead cats, hanging by a rope around their necks. Leon Katz in the living room, from the radiator pipe near the entrance. & cat-mother Catherine from the radiator pipe in the bedroom.
He must go back to the apartment and cut them down. & bury them in the garden. Under the big old cherry tree in the center on which they used to do their claws.

But if he goes back to the apartment he risks being seen by his wife. Who has taken a room in the home for friendless women across the street. A room with a street window facing the apartment entrance. She hasn't left the window since she took the room. & is waiting for him to come back. To string him up on the cherry tree in the garden, in celebration of his 45th birthday. Madness is giving her the muscles of a weightlifter.
She was already watching when he came home from his dinner with Patricia, well in time before midnight, with the champagne bottle under his arms. She followed him to the hotel & has made arrangements with the manager to keep him locked up in room 401 until he, too, becomes recognized. & goes stark raving mad from the uninterrupted applause of drilling outside the window   (Which is making the bed quake under him.)   for which the unexpectedly rich-&-recognized concert-harpist is paying 5 yellow-helmeted men

overtime, to keep drilling day & night, to keep him stimulated until he has finished writing his autobiography.

In the third person, to avoid problems with the I in identity. Perhaps in the second sex: The Autobiography of A Professional Seductress. A Life of Lies & Lays.

Which is *his* way of getting rid of the past.

It becomes an underground bestseller, after Women's Lib. puts it on its index. He'll make a grand living off his life. & live famously ever after, together with his almost-as-famous freckle-faced rusty-haired Irish concert-harpist wife. Maureen.

Whose one blueing tooth he can see, because she is smiling.

She is quoting a famous French author   whose name he has forgotten; he must ask Patricia to look it up for him   who said: "In an autobiography the author's imagination goes fishing for compliments."

But not in *his* autobiography. He has never suffered from an excess of imagination. Nor of originality. He has no specific talent. Only a number of better-than-average aptitudes. & a well-timed delivery that keeps his students from falling asleep. & would be a talent in a politician.

His wife is complimenting him on his honesty. Which she finds disarming.

'A lot of honest people lie to themselves all their lives,' he says to her. She smiles another blueing smile.

He had always thought that they had arrived at a fond understanding, after Leonora. That allowed him to see a girlfriend once in a while, while it gave her time to practice. (To the exclusion of cooking dinner. Of all wifely chores, except changing the litter in the cat box once a day.)

He'd always thought that she was a little grateful to him for postponing his own recognition   as a writer/painter/violinist/ etc./an archeologist, maybe; an architect, a master-builder; a politician. A prot.-no-pref. rep. for Dilettante Power   until she became a recognized concert-harpist.

But recognition has always been *his* hang-up. Much more than his wife's. Who is sitting on the edge of the bed, condescending with talent. She's not obsessed by the fear of mediocrity. & isn't trying a million different things, hoping to hit on an escape valve from the anonymous mold.

'Ambition makes bores': she says to him. How can he enjoy the ride if he's constantly fretting about getting there.

'What would he rather be?' she asks. 'Rich? Famous? Healthy? Beautiful? Or happy?'

She shakes her head at his answer that he'd rather be famous. 'But if you're happy you have everything!' she cries.

Doesn't she realize that he'd *be* happy if he were famous! & beautiful, automatically; one of the beautiful people. & probably also rich! That he cannot be happy as an anonymous professor of English Literature.

No; she doesn't. She has gone back to her harp.

Which she is perhaps practicing not so much in preparation for her recognition as not to hear him rehearse his third-person autobiographies/his paintings/concerts/buildings/excavations/psycho-social reforms, before he talks them to a variety of female listeners in preparation for bed.

'He who cultivates the inferior parts of his being is an inferior man.'

Doesn't she realize that fame means freedom! From ambition. From molds & comparisons.

'Fame is only a frame of reference': she says, with a bored blueing smile. Wanda Landowska may be famous to her, but to most baseball players she probably was just another Polish broad. With a pair of Klein's shopping bags for matched luggage.

& Baby Ruth was strictly a candy bar, to most harpists.

The famous authors he was forever quoting meant little to her most of the time. Meant to her mostly that he had little confidence in his own way of thinking. & expressing what he thought.

Did he really want to live 'in the public eye'? Exposed to red-rimmed indiscretion? & blood-shot greed?

Had his sister's example taught him nothing?

Did he want to be strip-teased by autograph maniacs & photograph maniacs & gum-shoed reporters every time he opened the door of their apartment? Did he want to be trailed every step to his girlfriends' apartments?

How does *he* know? He's never been in that position. She can't expect him to give up what he hasn't had. She doesn't know what she is talking about. She hasn't been exposed to a famous baby sister.

If he were famous   or at least recognized; as recognized as she became 10 days ago   he'd be free of the need for self-justification. He could hire some poor embittered who-are-you to write his autobiography for him. In the first person, in that case. For a phantom percentage of what he'd be raking in from the publisher. Since money flows to riches like water to wetness. Only the first million poses problems.

"If I were you, I'd be bored with myself too," one of his professors had said to him when he was an earnest college-18, & chronically worried about his marks. Good marks meant freedom; distinction from the acne-ed herd.

He had written a paper on Icarus for the professor, in which he had stressed the psychological ambiguity of the son's crashing into the sea when the sun melted the wings his father had fashioned for him. Not to fly higher than daddy with. While daddy's own wings held firm, all the middle-way from Crete to Sicily. For which he hoped to get an A, because his mother's psychiatrist, Dr. Catherine Spoon, had helped him write it.

He did get an A. & expressed such ambiguous gratitude that the professor invited him to dinner. Which the professor ordered from a deli, since he lived alone.

He was served a scrawny chicken wing   with reference to Icarus; because wings became youth better than an aging thigh   while the professor bit into the drumstick with grinning teeth.

Which later encouraged him, after dinner, to express his gratitude   also for future A's, perhaps   in a more tangibly affectionate classical-Greek fashion.

Which made him back out of the professor's house, away from the imprecation that he was boring. That the likes of him ought to be locked up in a closet, for coming on like a ton of pricks.

He had crept away, worried about his future marks.

On Dr. Spoon's consoling couch he had reverted to a device of his childhood. Which allowed him to unmake a mistake by projecting himself to a place where the clocks had not yet reached the time at which the mistake had been made. He had flown to San Francisco   in his head   where it was not yet 10 p.m.   where it was 7 p.m.   when no professor of ancient Greek had as yet found him boring for pressing his knees together like a Victorian prude to prevent a probing professorial hand from asserting itself between his worried adolescent thighs.

But San Francisco is west. & west is the future. Is autumn, & death. He must fly east, if he wants to unmake his mistakes. If he wants to cut his mediocrity at the roots.

He must fly against the sun. Deep into the past. & keep flying faster & faster; without stopping until his past materializes under the pressure of his speed & he can see it lying below like a landscape of cobwebs & chicken coops & barbed-wired play pens. & milestoned mud.

& somewhere in the French-Greek-German-Danish-Irish-British-American underbrush a white-haired flower of universal love. A dandelion. Which the Patrician French call Piss-in-Bed. & eat as a salad.

The wind plays darts with its seeds, which prick the hide of divisive egotism.

To avoid the delay of purchasing a ticket to a random eastern destination to Paris, as a tribute to Patricia; for lack of a more exotic geographical imagination & to cut down on the hassle of having to intimidate a number of unabashed fellow travellers & professionally seductive stewardesses he hi-jacks the first private plane he sees standing on the runway, ready to take off.

For Vietnam, he discovers. On a private peace mission, with a cargo of mickey-mouse watches.

The owner-pilot is a young millionaire by the name of Chrys Cronyn. Who is the age of the son he has not had; just old enough to die in Vietnam. & looks disconcertingly like his Irish concert-harpist wife Maureen, except for a joint drooling from his mouth. & longer reddish hair.

He might be his concert-harpist wife Maureen's Irish-looking son. By a Mr. Cronyn whom she's never mentioned. On whom she walked out   without her baby son; with her harp   although Mr. Cronym had not been unfaithful   to become a concert-harpist.

To whom she has gone back now that she's become recognized. Without the cats. Mr. Cronyn was already allergic to cats when she left him.

Perhaps Chrys Cronyn is her illegitimate son. Whom she abandoned in the home for friendless women in which she'd given birth. Which a friendless millionairess had founded as a tax deduction. & the friendless millionairess adopted the little bastard.

Perhaps his wife Maureen sold her son to Miss Cronyn or to a son-less couple of millionaires by the same name   for the price of a concert-harp.

He realizes that he knows very little about his wife's love life before their marriage. He knows only that she was not a virgin when they first made love. Not that he had expected her to be a virgin, at close to 30, when they first made love. In spite of her being Irish; & playing the harp. Under a potted palm in a French restaurant   a different French restaurant   where he first saw her. Projecting an image of patched purity & drooping Icarus wings.

Perhaps she has abandoned more than one orphan to the potluck of the Irish, in order to be a harpist rather than a mother. Other sons who've had to make their own motherless millions.

Chrys Cronyn has earned his money. Playing Orphan Annie on nation-wide TV in drag under an assumed name. Now he wants to be a saint, under his own name, to honor the father & mother he's never known. Preach childlike simplicity, & spend what he has earned on bringing peace to the world. Beginning with Vietnam.

He counts on winning the Indo-Chinese over to the American way of life by bombing both sides with mickey-mouse watches. Which will subtly disconnect them from the Chinese calendar; which is in the year of the Rat. Once they're hooked on good time play-time USA, they won't want to continue dying for survival. They won't want to fight other nations' economic battles in their rice paddies. Hanoi & Saigon will shake hands. Surrender to each other, & go on welfare.

He has faith in the child in man, regardless of race, creed, or calendar. He has yet to meet a man who doesn't enjoy taking a watch apart.

It doesn't take long to convince Chrys Cronyn to keep a straight eastern course. & to keep flying faster & faster non-stop against time, when he realizes that he might perhaps drop his watches before the hostilities started in Vietnam. That he might perhaps prevent them from starting by dropping his watches. & change the course of history.

He becomes extremely excited at the thought of flying still faster, further & further back. Far enough to interfere with the Crucifixion, perhaps. & still further back, all the way to the beginning. Deep into the Old Testament. To the second if not the first original mistake. & perhaps distract Cain from slaying Abel by a well-timed drop of a mickey-mouse watch into the angrily raised not yet murderous fist.

Of 2 well-timed mickey-mouse watches, to give Abel no cause to become jealous of Cain, & perhaps repeat ancient history in reverse.

& of course they'll film everything. & televise it world-wide, for people to see where & when what went wrong. & to realize that it has now been corrected. & that they no longer have any hereditary excuse for killing each other.

S T O P !

He has just realized that the millionaire-pilot is a girl.

A young millionairess by the name of Chrys Cronyn who looks disconcertingly like his Irish concert-harpist wife Maureen, except for a half-smoked joint drooling from her mouth. & might be his wife Maureen's Irish-looking daughter from her previous marriage to Mr. Cronyn. Or . . . & . . . etc. . . . about all of which he knows nothing.

Chrys Cronyn could of course also be the daughter he has not had. Except that she's not beautiful enough. Any daughter of his would have inherited his Irish-beauty mother's eyes & teeth. Not his Irish harpist-wife's hair and freckles. Unless she is a spiteful daughter, spitefully taking after his baby sister, her slimmed-down aunt, & is on her way to become a buddhist nun, in Vietnam.

But that is unlikely. He has never thought of himself as the father of a daughter. To avoid the temptation of incest which society expects of the youthful-looking father of a daughter.

Even Dr. Spoon used to admit that he didn't turn on to family ties.

Miss Cronyn is less childlike & less saintly than the former drag-orphan. & has no desire to withdraw from the scene now that she has finally come into her millions. After Daddy Warbucks-Cronyn finally succumbed to apoplexy.

She is flying to Vietnam to add a few personal shots to her collection of battle paintings & war-horror photographs. & puts up no resistance   but becomes extremely excited   at the prospect of taking her own pictures of the second world war. & of the Spanish civil war.

Of shooting the American civil war, maybe. & maybe Waterloo   Austerlitz   Hastings, if she flies fast enough. & keeps flying   faster & faster   non-stop against time.

Of shooting Issus, maybe. All the way back to 333 B.C.

The only battle date he remembers. When Alexander defeated Darius III. Who was destroying a great empire, as the oracle had told him he would. Without specifying that the great empire would be his own.

He remembers Issus because of the oracle. Ambiguity already held a fascination for him in highschool.

When he had wanted to be a hero, like the rest of the conformist herd. & had envied Alexander   & Napoleon the Great Peter   the dandelion-hearted Richard. Who had lived in heroic times, when it was easy to be a hero. Unlike 1937/38, when nobody was a hero. At least not in Pennsylvania, U.S.A.

He'd have been a greater hero. A hypnotist, like Rasputin. Only greater. *He* would have *talked* to the enemy. His deep heroic voice booming out over the battle fields, & everywhere white makeshift flags   handkerchiefs; a woman's petticoat would have shot up & waved surrender.

He would not have lost at Waterloo.

History as he learned it then runs through his memory like a broad country road. With war heroes & conquerors' statues for milestones. Between which lie boring little grass patches of peace.

He had wanted to become a historian, in highschool.

They have completed their 401st time around when he begins to perceive himself.

Or rather, he perceives an imprint in the atmosphere that has his shape & movements. The mold cast by a person's passage through time, which remains after Killjoy leaves, after George Washington wakes up & moves on.

His mold is retracing his steps of the night before. It is backing away from the hotel entrance, across the quaking plank which bridges the gap that has been drilled into the sidewalk. Down the familiar streets which he walked the night before   at a fast pace   which accelerates as he approaches the door of his apartment & culminates in a backward hop down the 3 entrance steps.

His neighborhood church strikes the first quarter after midnight. He spins around to face the door, & goes through the locking gestures in reverse. Starting with the alarm lock at the bottom   the center lock   the off-center lock   the top lock. Unlocking what he hopes he locked the night before.

He thinks he did. Mechanically. He usually is mechanically cautious. He'll find out soon enough, when he goes back to the apartment.

His wife is sitting cross-legged on top of a suitcase in the middle of yesterday's living room floor. Offering closed eyelids to the afternoon ceiling. Leon Katz runs to her & climbs into her triangled lap. Her right hand detaches itself from her right knee, detaches thumb from index finger, & scratches the furry rust-red throat. 2 tears gather in the nose corners of her closed lids. Quicksilver down her cheeks & meet at the chin.
"Don't!" he shouts to her. "Don't kill the things we love! I'll make you happy, if recognition isn't making you happy. Patricia can finish her thesis without me. I'll drop her, & start practicing the violin again."
She doesn't hear him.
He wants to bail out & run to her. But if he stops flying east & floats down vertically, he'll be back in the present before his parachute has time to unfold. He'll come too late to prevent her mistake.
He borrows one of the saintly Chrys Cronyn's mickey-mouse watches. & aims it at his wife's harp which is leaning against the living room couch. There is a strident sound: from a broken string.
His wife later uses it to string up Leon Katz & Catherine.

Meanwhile, the young Irish-looking millionaire twins have been flying faster. Back into their own much briefer past. They're standing in the dingy yard of a tenement, an orphaned static 8 years old, with ribbon-tied bobbed hair, wagging knowing fingers at a grinning brillo-furred mutt.

He passes them on his backward way to Leonora's house. Before he is sucked into the sour-smelling graffiti-walled tunnel of Leonora's hall, & races up the 5 flights of stairs which he raced down 8 or 9 years ago, after he broke up with Leonora.

He backs into Leonora's studio, into the parting scene she made him.

Her wide blue eyes are swollen shut from crying. She is holding a baby-sized rag doll by the throat. Which she has made of the pants & the shirt he had left at her studio. For her to wear, & paint in. Which he had worn while he painted his cat while she painted him painting.

The doll's face is the larger part of a broken record. Of the song to which they used to dance, in the studio, after they were through painting. Presley's wooden-heart song: 'Love me right . . . love me good . . .' She has painted a woman's face on it which looks disconcertingly like the Irish face of his concert-harpist wife Maureen. Surrounded by dishevelled reddish-brown leather fringes.

The resemblance disconcerts him all the more since Leonora has never met his wife. Nor has she seen a photograph of her. He's not the family-in-wallet type.

The doll's body is bristling with hairpins & sewing needles. "I'll kill her!" hiccoughs Leonora. "I'll throttle her! I'll string her up!"

Why had he wanted to make love to *her* if he loves his wife?

He can't answer her question. He doesn't know himself. Because he's never sure that he can do it again after he's done it, perhaps. Which is why he keeps testing.

Thoughtless gluttony, more likely . . .

Thoughtless gluttony used to be his Leo-mother's excuse when she returned from having sung herself into   & out of some man's bed. While his Danish-sentimental father suffered. & blamed himself for not being financially potent enough to move to a big city. Where his mother could have had adequate singing lessons. Which was all she lacked to become a star.

Instead of writing her off with a scarlet letter across her breasts. & making the money he blamed himself for lacking with an updated unexpurgated version of the potboiler he was living. On the dark side of the could-be star.

To him she *was* a star: his father used to say.

He used to think that his father was a sap. A caterpillar married to a butterfly. A dull mediocre highschool teacher in Nowhere, Pennsylvania.

To whom the butterfly remained a star until the day she died. Of the thoughtless gluttony which was also her excuse when she had smoked too much. & felt pulling pains in her legs that made it hard for her to sit still. To lie still, & fall asleep.

She had died as ego-dramatically as she had lived. Crawling out from under her oxygen tent in the hospital after the nurse left the room. Sitting at her own bedside shrugging off his father's frantic protestations lighting a cigarette . . .

He can't remember who said that few men made it beyond their father's potential. Dr. Spoon, perhaps. At least he's not teaching highschool in Pennsylvania. Where his retired father is still blaming himself for the loss of his unfaithful wife. Writing uncommercial free-verse lamentations to her memory.

Which his recently recognized concert-harpist wife is setting to music.

His wife & his father are sitting in the living room of his boyhood, each in a corner of the shabbily slip-covered couch.

His father is reciting his latest lament while she improvises a melody for it on her harp.

Because his wife has gone to see his father, in Pennsylvania. To ask his father's permission to kill his only son. To avenge the murder of her love.

Which can't have been true love, if it has been killed. True love is immortal: declares his father, surprisingly witholding his permission.

Which his wife is trying to cajole out of him, with her music.

She has never particularly liked his father. But couldn't think of anybody else to whom she could complain about him. She thought he'd understand. She hadn't expected competition for the martyr's crown of horns.

—But at least your wife felt guilty when she came back from her flings: she argues. She didn't try to convince you that she was normal, & that you were not.

—& she didn't bring her men home to you to befriend. To make amends for your existence. & make them applaud your concerts, to make amends for *their* existence . . .

It was his tragically unapplauded wife   not he   who had given concerts: his father points out. Tragically few concerts. Unlike their tragically over-applauded teenage daughter, the one-time rock singer & current nun.

His wife would have been *grateful* to have been applauded: he says.

His wife certainly *deserved* to be applauded. She was a star: he says.

True love is independent of whatever the beloved person may or may not do: he says: That is, after all, part of the beloved character.

His wife likes his father less & less. Yach: she thinks. You really asked for it, brother. Father. You win.

But *she* didn't ask for it. She finds no inspiration in loving a thoughtless glutton. Who nibbles his way through life, causing pain to anyone who is gullible enough to feed him. Because he's too greedy to make a choice, & forego all the other beckoning snacks.

She should never have gone back to him, after she'd walked out that first time. Because of Leonora. (Who had wanted to walk out of life because of her.) She should have realized that he'd start nibbling elsewhere, sooner or later.

She'll kill him yet, when she gets back from Pennsylvania. With or without his father's permission.

Why should sharing love with more than one partner produce such pain? He loves both his wife & Leonora. Differently, but equally sincerely. He has never been insincere in bed. Why do they both feel deprived?

'Because he's been confusing love with lust,' replies his wife of not quite 3 years.

She is standing in the bathroom of a midtown French restaurant, in front of the mirror, hypnotizing herself into going back out into the dining room to continue playing her harp.

'How would *he* feel if she told him she'd been going to bed with the headwaiter?' she asks him.

'He'd feel that she might have picked the manager,' he says superciliously. While a doubt shoots through him. & with the doubt a pain. A double pain: of humiliation mixed with a feeling of loss.

Miss C. Cronyn is shooting the Battle of the Bulge.

He is an earnest college-18, & makes a point of holding her camera for her, so that she can keep flying   faster & faster   while she shoots. He'd rather not dwell on his humiliating exit from the ancient-Greek professor's house.

Her saintly brother is getting ready to prevent Pearl Harbor. With a hailstorm of mickey-mouse watches.

His sister tries to prevent him from preventing Pearl Harbor. Which would deprive her of one of her most dramatically personal collector's items. A hitherto undocumented moment of truth. Which she is thinking of sending to the White House. Or to the New York Times.

She blocks the release hatch with her left knee & thigh. Her brother tries to pry her loose. Neither is paying attention to the flying. They're slipping back. Forward in time.

Pain is useful, smiles Dr. Catherine Q. Spoon. It serves as a memory peg. Especially pains of humiliation. They stand like milestones   taller than moments of triumph   along the somnambulant road to consciousness.

He can't bear to go through that humiliating experience again. He is *not* boring. Or dull. Or mediocre. He makes Miss Cronyn sit up straight in the pilot seat. She bites his hands on her shoulders, but steps on the gas. A drizzle of mickey-mouse watches falls over Pennsylvania.

One of them bounces off the balding head of his father who is bending over his baby-sister's crib, with a bottle in his hand.

It distracts his father from asking the thick-braided German babysitter why she has again neglected to give the baby her bottle. Why she's always letting the baby cry until she's blue in the face.

'What the hell was that?' he asks instead, rubbing his bald spot. Looking around the ceiling for a piece of fallen plaster.

The babysitter giggles. Instead of blushing & repeating last week's stammered lie-excuse: that the baby had been fast asleep until 2 minutes ago.

He hopes he will never be a balding boring dupe like his father.

He quickly reaches over the saintly brother's shoulder & drops another watch into the wicker basket on the babysitter's German brother's bicycle. Which has been trailing him all the way to school. He suspects that the babysitter has maybe told her brother what they do together while his baby sister cries herself blue in the face.

The brother snatches up the watch. Holds it close to his eyes. Holds it up to his right ear. To his left ear. Grins. Straps it onto his wrist. 'Gee, thanks!' he yells, & pedals off.

Instead of cornering him in the school yard, gripping his shirt collar with a white-knuckled fist, & informing him through clenched teeth that nobody but nobody but brother gets inside his sister. Or else!

He could skip school. Run home & pull the babysitter by her braid until she falls down on top of him some more. But he's already too young. His famous baby sister has not yet been born. To cement his parents' marriage together again.

He is 7 years old. He is sitting at the dining table in his grandparents' house in Intercourse, Pennsylvania, working at adding 99 plus 99. Under a green porcelain lampshade with long dishevelled rusty-red fringes. Which feel like flies in his hair every time he moves his head.

His mother is bending over him with a cigarette drooling from her mouth. Which she doesn't take out to tell him that the easy way to add 99 plus 99 is to add 100 plus 100, & then take off 2.

Cigarette smoke is in his eyes. He thinks his mother is full of tricks.

The millionaire twins are quarreling again. About an antisemitic housepainter who is making a speech in Munich, Germany. Under the assumed name of Hitler, instead of Hister, as predicted by Nostradamus.

The saintly brother wants to drown the housepainter out & ridicule him once & for all by dropping a mickey-mouse watch into each listener's raised right hand.

Which would invalidate his sister's almost complete collection of concentration camp photographs, & reduce them to the level of phantasy. Of exaggerated horror stills.

If they continue to pay no attention to where they're going, he'll have to ask them to leave the flying to him.

. . . Which they'll be only too happy to do. If he's elected pilot, after they vote on it . . .: they say politely. . . . By secret ballot . . .: they smile. Winking at each other. Sure of their majority, like the parents of an only child.

Too late. They have collided with a rainbow.

The jolt projects him back into his mother's womb. He feels permeated with the unfulfilled desire to become a famous singer. An opera star.

He understands in a flash that the millionaire twins are not his concert-harpist wife's Irish-looking children whom she sacrificed to become recognized. Nor are they the children he has not had. They are his parents. His Irish-beauty Leo-mother. . . . Who looks less beautiful at 20, than when he saw her on her deathbed . . . Who often quarreled with his then not yet balding saintly sentimental Pisces-sap of a father. Who feels too young to become a father. But thinks that a little son or a little daughter would console his wife after the disappointment of her first & only audition in a big concert hall in New York City, 10 days ago. When she had cried all the way home to Pennsylvania, until her wide blue eyes looked like welts, after being told that she had a nice voice, but needed more practice.

He also thinks that a grandson a grandchild of any sex might reconcile his prominent Protestant parents who do not look kindly upon an Irish Catholic daughter-in-law. Who moreover ambitions to be an opera singer. Whose father had moreover been their mailman.

He hopes that a grandchild will dispose them more generously toward their talented but financially mediocre son.

Who gives up writing & becomes a highschool teacher, after the birth of his son.

Knowing what he knows he tries to discourage the millionaire twins from making love. Right in front of him. Precariously, in the skidding plane.

He begs them to use birthcontrol, at least. They needn't feel concerned about his new life. He's in no hurry. He'll be glad to wait another 7 or 8 years longer. Until he can be born famous, like his ungrateful baby sister. (He would not become a nun!)

They don't listen to him.

They're quarreling about who should climb on top of whom, in the narrow pilot seat.

There is a shadowy reddish-brown flash. They must have crashed & are all dead. All 3 of them.

He is definitely dead. To be looking into a beautiful garden on the other side of a silent red stone wall. He can't help looking into the garden, & must have been placed in whatever position he is in, in order to realize that he has not been admitted. That he is at present in hell.

His wife Maureen must also be dead. Perhaps the 2 junkies did kill her after all & stuffed her into the garbage cabinet under the kitchen sink where he didn't look last night. Where her stiffened body lies wedged between the water pipes & can't be pulled out until decay sets in & makes her flexible again.

He can see her sitting under the big old cherry tree in the center. Which is in full bloom. Her reddish hair is flowing to her shoulders like liquid sunshine. Her skin is a freckle-less procelain white. She looks more beautiful than his mother looked on her deathbed. She is playing her harp, & their 2 cats are dancing to the music.

On the highest cherry blossom a hand-sized royal blue butterfly is dipping rhythmic wings.

He wants to run to the foot of the silent wall & try to scale it. To explain to her that it has all been a misunderstanding. Which is irrevocable only if she insists. He hadn't realized how selfish he'd been. What a thoughtless glutton.

But he is 3 or 4 stories up in the air, & he doesn't know how to get down. Perhaps his falling body got caught in a 3-or-4-storey-high tree, when they crashed, for the sole fiendish purpose of torturing him with the constant view of inaccessible beauty.

But there is dirty glass in front of his eyes. & his legs won't move. They are thin & weak, one shorter than the other. He can't stand on them.

He is sitting at a third-or-fourth-floor window, in a wheel chair. There is snow on the outer ledge, & also on top of the silent red stone wall. The sky is a murky grey, except over the garden where the sun is shining. He feels cold & clammy. The blanket has slipped off his knees. Which look like door knobs.

He has a reddish-brown skirt on. & when he lifts it up to look underneath, he sees that he is a girl. 8 or 9 years old.

She has been looking out the window all day. Since 8 o'clock that morning, when her Uncle Healey lifted her out of her bed & wrapped her in a blanket & set her down in the wheelchair at the window, before he left for work.

Her Uncle Healey is an electrician. & not really her uncle. She just calls him uncle because her mother used to call him uncle, although he wasn't her mother's uncle either.

'Uncle Healey lights the lights', her mother used to say.

At 10 o'clock the woman next door came over & held her under the faucet in the kitchen. & pulled the reddish-brown skirt over her head. & made her eat.

She hates eating. Especially the chewy stuff. She'd much rather just drink, like her Uncle Healey. But the woman next door won't let her. Sometimes she squeezes her mouth open with one hand & shoves a piece of meat in with the other. "If you don't eat, you can't get well," she says. "You hardly weigh more than a cat."

The woman's hands always smell of onion.

She knows she'd get well if she could sit in the beautiful garden. Where it's never winter. Always spring & summer, spring & summer. But if she asks the woman next door to wheel her there, she'll tell the other neighbors about the garden. & they'll start throwing old light bulbs & shoes & empty beer cans over the silent red wall. & maybe hit her mother on the head.

Her mother is sitting down there in the garden. Under the big cherry tree in the center; she is waving to her to come on down & play with the 2 cats. & with the big blue butterfly that was once a little green caterpillar named Beaufort. Who didn't believe in butterflies.

Her mother has a story to tell about Beaufort. It's called: The Little Caterpillar Who Didn't Believe In Butterflies. & it is dedicated to Miss Deborah Blossom.

"Beaufort was a beautiful little caterpillar.

He had fluffy green shiny fur. & hundreds of pairs of nimble feet of a lighter green on which he'd run up & down the branches of the cherry tree to peek under the leaves, & into the blossoms.

'You're getting to be quite a big caterpillar', one of the cherry blossoms said to him. The top blossom, whose name was Deborah. 'Before you know it you'll have turned into a big beautiful butterfly.'

'I will not!' cried Beaufort. 'There are no butterflies. I've never seen one. They don't exist. They are the ghosts of poor dead caterpillars.'

'In that case you'll soon turn into a big beautiful ghost,' laughed Deborah Blossom.

& all the other blossoms started laughing too.

'I don't believe in ghosts,' said Beaufort angrily. 'It's all in your imagination. Just because you like to have your pollen tickled.'

The cherry blossoms blushed. & giggled. & laughed some more.

'But you can't just refuse to grow up,' they said.

'I *am* grown up,' said Beaufort, 'as grown up as I'll ever be.'

'I'll show you,' he said. 'I'll tickle your pollen for you.'

& he began marching all over them with his hundreds of pairs of nimble light-green feet.

'Ouch! Stop! Enough!' they all cried breathlessly. 'Stop that nonsense & grow up! What would you say if all of us refused to become cherries?'

'I don't care what all of you refuse to do as long as you don't mention those you-know-whats to me,' he said.

'But butterflies are beautiful,' said the cherry blossoms. 'All flowers love butterflies.'

'B...B...B...B...B...B...B...Butt...Butt... Butter...,' said Beaufort.

He was so angry, he couldn't speak. He crawled under a leaf & spun himself into a tent.

When he came out again he had turned into a big beautiful royal blue butterfly.

All the cherry blossoms applauded. & started to sing:

'Caterpillar sheds its skin
To find a butterfly within...'

Beaufort realized that they were singing about him, but he didn't understand what they were singing. He had forgotten that he had been a caterpillar. He didn't know they existed. He hadn't seen one yet."

    The little girl has disappeared.
    Perhaps she has died plunging from her third-or-fourth-storey window into the beautiful garden.
    Which has also disappeared.
    Unless it had never been there, & she had only imagined it. & had driven her Uncle Healey stark raving mad, asking him every night to carry her downstairs in her blanket & lift her over the silent red stone wall. Until he had finally opened the window, one night, when he had come home from the bar later & drunker than usual, & had tilted the wheelchair over the snow-covered ledge & poured her out. & she had floated down into the garden on the magic carpet of her blanket. Or else, without the blanket, her reddish-brown skirt billowing about her uneven legs like a parachute.

    Unless she hasn't been born yet. Which is more logical, since they're flying backwards in time. Against the sun; in the opposite direction of chronology.

    Because they're still flying. The Irish-faced millionaire twins still in the pilot seat, one astride the other in a Siamese twine, manipulating dual controls.
    Their plane didn't crash when he thought they had crashed when he saw the shadowy reddish-brown flash. Which had merely been a rough splice between lives.

    He is between lives once more.
    He is the transilient soul he sees hovering in front of the Relocation Center Information booth.

"Is a change of sex permitted?" he hears it ask. In a choking English male voice which has not yet shed the mold of its last personality.

"Wherever customs permit it," he hears the voiceless language-less reply.

He feels the urge to ask what exactly is meant by 'customs'. Does it mean that a soul remains subject to the local laws & social attitudes of its last incarnation, & is allowed to switch from a male to a female body   or from a female to a male body   only in areas & eras that don't consider one sex human, & the other sub-human   or animal   or impure & frown upon transmigrants?

If so, he would like to enter into an argument with the voice-less language-less informant inside the booth. & question the post-mortem validity of social customs in general. & in particular of customs that make moral value distinctions between purely amoral principles, such as: masculine & feminine, positive & negative, etc. Which are equally indispensable to the production of life. Of light.

How can a soul be expected to understand both sides of the coin   & ultimately integrate   if reincarnation perpetuates dualism? he feels the urge to ask.

He probably did ask just that, at the time. & received the invalid little girl's body in reply.

"Don't insist!" he shouts to his hovering transilient soul. "Don't be curious! Remember, curiosity kills cats!"

It doesn't hear his well-meant warning. It hears only voiceless language-less commands. Matter has no impact on it. The well-aimed mickey-mouse watch which he tosses down to distract it from entering into an argument with the universal principle bounces off & returns to his hand.

To his left hand. Although he used his right hand to throw it, as he normally does.

The master-printer, leveller, & ladies' man Beaufort

Hookker   Mr. Bô, as he is known to most early-to-mid-17th-century inhabitants of York, NE England   is left-handed.

Or rather: Beaufort Hookker *was* left-handed up to his premature demise on the evening of March 23, 1648, at 9 p.m. On the eve of his 45th birthday.

When several mid-17th-century Yorkers   suspicious husbands & equally suspicious fathers of adolescent daughters   contrived his execution. In retaliation for fines they had paid for beating their wives &/or adolescent daughters after 9 p.m. When a recent law forbade the beating of wives &/or daughters. Between the hours of 9 p.m. to 5 a.m., when beating them was considered a disturbance rather than a keeping of the peace, under the recent law.

Which most male mid-17th-century Yorkers resented. As a curtailment of their 'true liberty'. Which intended a man's wife   children/servants/gods   to be his own. For him to deal with as he saw fit.

& they suspected the master-printer & militant leveller   the arrogant Mr. Bô   of having denounced them for post-9-p.m.-beating of the wives &/or adolescent daughters of whom he had given them reason to become suspicious.

Their united resentment succeeded in having him hanged. As a papist. Which was one of the few remaining expedients to hang a man who was neither a pauper nor a vagrant nor a common thief, in socializing mid-17th-century England. Where artisans & tradesmen were beginning to raise not only their middle-class heads, but also their voices.

Modern religious tolerance did not extend to papists.

The master-printer's booming leveller's voice, denouncing the Commonwealth's repressive policy in Ireland, took on a devious ring when it was whispered that he used to have an Irish wife   with freckles & reddish witch's hair   who had abruptly disappeared from York 10 or more years ago. To return to Ireland. Where her plotting papist husband had sent her. In good time to help him foment the Irish rebellion in

November 1641. Which cost hundreds   perhaps thousands of English lives.

& made the Judas rich.

What honest printer could afford to replace all his pewter mugs with glass?

Many Yorkers   who were not all husbands &/or fathers-of-adolescent-daughters; or who had as yet had no reason to suspect & beat their wives &/or adolescent daughters before or after 9 p.m.   had seen & admired the printer's new drinking glasses when they had gone to his shop to pick up a pamphlet he'd printed.

& sometimes also written.

The glasses were more tangible & admirable than the loving forgiveness of a jilted husband who overcomes justified resentment for his   indeed Irish, & freckle-faced, & red-haired; ex-Catholic   wife who walked out on him 11 years ago.

(He'd always thought husbands walked out on wives, not wives on husbands.)

Less than a year after the birth of his 7th daughter. Patricia. As soon as P. had been old enough to be weaned. Although he had never beaten his wife   or any of his 7 daughters   either after or before 9 p.m., & might conceivably have extended his justified resentment to all of Ireland.

Where his run-away wife is probably indeed living. If she's still alive.

In a convent, maybe. If she's gone back to her family faith.

Under a new family-nameless name: Sister Mary. Mother Carey. To purge her identity of the chattel name of Hookker. Doing penitence for having had a Protestant husband for close to 7 years. For having borne 7 Protestant daughters   her 7 lively sins   2 of them twins.

Unless she's living in a coven, if she's still alive. Under another assumed misogamous name. Semantha, maybe. Anathema. Anapest. Which would be more in keeping with her red-haired freckle-faced faith. & is spending her days her nights brewing bitter resentment potions against the husband she walked out on.

Taking nothing but her cat. A coal-black kitten born the same day as his 7th daughter Patty. With the single perfect-white hair which coal-black cats allegedly conceal somewhere in their blackness. Which one must find, & pluck, for luck. Which she is wearing in a locket on her throat.

The by-now-almost-12-year-old cat is sitting crouched on her shoulder, glowing charcoal eyes into the misty Irish night. Adding its venomous spit to the potion she is brewing. With herbs she has gathered behind the castle ruin in which she lives. With other red-haired freckle-faced Irish witches with spitting black cats on their shoulders. Who are helping her stir. Who are all patiently poisoning the lives of husbands they walked out on.

Perhaps she would not have walked out if he had beaten her when she threatened to walk out, shortly after Patty was born. Instead of asking if she wasn't at all curious to watch little Patty grow. & didn't she think their 7 daughters needed their mother to grow up properly?
But corporal punishment is against his leveller's principles. He has even stopped beating his servants.
He probably should have beaten her nonetheless when she replied that she wasn't presumptuous enough to think that *her* mistakes would be less harmful to their daughters' upbringing than his. Or some other woman's. His stout childless sister's, for instance, who had never made a mistake, all her prosperous tavern-owning life.
He should have tied her to the bedpost by her freckled wrists & beaten her black & blue. It probably would have meant to her that he loved her more than his principles. That

he was not ranking her on a level with the maids he had stopped beating.

Whom she continued to beat. In open defiance of his principles. His 'equality-nonsense'. Which she refused to believe that he believed. Which was a slap in the face of nature. Where everything was based on hierarchy. Where a mouse was a mouse, & a cat a cat. & neither ambitioned to accede to the other's level.

& wasn't he the first to make distinctions? Between males & females, for instance? & didn't the distinction automatically prompt a difference in treatment?

He was behaving exactly like a certain constipated German monk who had shelved the saints & demoted the Virgin, in order to let his self-indulgence grant him remission & marry a nun.

Exactly like a certain blue-bearded king who latched on to the ex-monk's principles in order to unmarry his queens. "Ennery the Heighth I ham I ham . . ."

Was he hoping to elevate his own station by abolishing the ranks of the higher-born? she asked. Tartly affirming that the 'e' in equality stood for abolishment of quality. In front of their grinning servants. Who respected her more than they respected him, since she was still beating them.

She liked to use them as an audience, at meal times, when she chided him for not practicing the equality he preached when it came to raising their 7 daughters. Whom he did not love all equally well. Nagging him for preferring chubby friendly Carey   their second   to the older sterner Kate. & to Deborah   their third. The most beautiful of the 7. As beautiful as glass; but remote.

Why did he permit Leonora   their fourth   to paint landscapes & creatures of her fancy into the first letters of chapters when neither Kate nor Carey nor Deborah was allowed to touch his paints & brushes?

& why was he forever kissing baby Patty when he hardly ever kissed the twins?

Perhaps she had not walked out. & is dead.
Perhaps Bô Hookker beat his wife to death when she threatened to walk out on him   on his papist plottings   one sudden evening 11 years ago. 7 years before the post-9 p.m.-anti-wife-beating law was put into effect.
More & more mid-17th-century neighbors   male as well as female; especially female   began recalling more & more vividly that they had heard a commotion in the printer's house, 11 years ago. On a cold evening. Sometime during the winter of 1636, the early spring of 1637. When they had also seen a light flicker in the print shop, later, late during the night. & had wondered what urgent pamphlet the dedicated printer might be printing, so late into the night. . . . When the levelling liar had probably been busy heating water on his stove in the print shop, to thaw the NE English winter ground before he buried his dead wife   in the cold light of the moon   under the oldest sturdiest cherry tree in the center of his orchard.
Where her body had perhaps been lying all these 11 years. Her bones intertwined with the roots of the tree. Which have adjusted their growth to her position.
For 11 NE English summers Bô Hookker   & his 7 motherless daughters   & his readily changing maids   have been eating plump yellow cherries that had perhaps nourished their juicy flesh on the flesh of the wife he murdered.
Who had perhaps not been completely dead when he buried her. Perhaps she had only fainted under his cruel beatings, & the papist monster had buried her alive, under his cherry tree in his orchard.

He still misses her.

He misses the food she used to cook. & spice with herbs she used to grow around the fruit trees in his orchard.

Not one of his 7 daughters has learned how to cook. They've all learned to set type. Even Patty who is only 11; who'll be a lanky 12 next month reads letters upside down. For years she's been reading mom like wow.

For 11 years he's been eating nothing but servants' food. Which always has a greasy taste of duty. Of joylessness & lack of love. Even if he takes one of them to his bed, occasionally. Sleeping with the cook does not improve the soup.

It grieves him to think that his run-away wife probably still resents him. If she's still alive. If she's found a way to stay alive without him, with her herbs & her tricks.

With some new man, probably. Who's too self-satisfied to be ambitious. Too unimaginative to tell a lie. Who rarely looks at other women because he basically doesn't like women. Not any more than his run-away wife basically likes men.

Or women.

Or children.

Which her new man isn't man enough to make. Which is why she likes him. They like each other for the things they dislike about life. At least the human manifestation of life. They both have a passion for herbs. & flog each other regularly with fresh nettles every night before they go to bed, as proof of their passion.

They don't care about what happens to England. Or to Ireland. They think the future of mankind is no concern of theirs. They're the living end.

His wife would probably laugh out loud if she knew that the glorious historic future to which he has always felt predestined by his birthday: March 24, 1603, the day on which Queen Elizabeth died   is about to be ungloriously unhistorically curtailed. On the eve of his 45th birthday. At 9 p.m. That he is about to be hanged for having been her husband.

Which he never should have been. She should have known better than to get herself entangled with an early Aries. Whose blunt fire risked scorching her Taurus earth: she tells him. Her Irish freckle-face aged by 11 years of relentless resentment. Still bull-headedly clinging to her belief in astrology. Which her more enlightened contemporaries have dropped to the level of superstition.

'They're replacing knowledge with science': she smiles. Revealing a set of blueing teeth. She shrugs. She'll go on gathering her herbs according to the phases of the moon. They're welcome to compare the potency of her potions.

She might have spared herself a lot of humiliation if she had heeded the advice of the stars instead of marrying him: she says. She walked into the trap with her eyes wide open, telling herself that she was marrying the exception. Because he had worked so hard at seducing her.

That's what she's been resenting all these years: her own open-eyed stupidity . . .

Because his wife has come back to York for the occasion of his hanging. About which she read in the sky. In the moon nearly at the full.

She wants to witness the 'liar's moment of truth'. She wants to watch his face

(which has aged much less, by comparison with hers. Less resentfully. His skin is as fair & smooth as it was 11 years ago. "Like a green apple that would rather rot than ripen": she cackles . . .)

as it is being pushed through a noose by 5 retaliating mid-17th-century wife-beaters. In preparation for stringing him

up on the oldest sturdiest cherry tree in his orchard behind the print shop. Under a cold full NE English moon.
"A ram butts into a noose & gets its horns entangled": she cackles. Linking arms with the wives & daughters he had tried to protect from being beaten after 9 p.m.
His wife has linked arms with his stout childless sister whom she has never particularly liked. Who has closed her prosperous tavern for the duration of his hanging.
The women are forming a circle around the tree & around the silent huddle of his 7 soon-to-be-fatherless daughters at the foot of the tree   in anticipation of dancing around his slow-swaying body. Of lifting their skirts & chanting:

> Mr. Bô dångles . . .
> Mr. Bô dångles . . .

She doesn't recognize Patty   whom she hasn't seen since P. was an 11-month-old baby; who'll be a lanky 12 years old next month   who manages to crawl through the circling forest of impatient female legs.
Patty is planning to set fire to the print shop. She hopes that it will spread to the neighboring houses. To her fat aunt's tavern, if the wind picks up. If she's lucky the whole city of York, NE England, will burn. & she'll skip rope over the smoking rubble & recite the alphabet upside down.

The ubiquitous millionaire twins crawl through after her.
They're a wise mid-17th-century 13, named Honor & Charity. Still reddish-haired & Irish-faced, but not rich.
At least not yet.
& not yet orphaned. Although they're acting as though they'd never had a father. As though what is about to happen in the cherry orchard behind their crawling backs concerned them only insofar as it will leave them free to travel.

To hike to London. To lie in the less-&-less safe London streets, together with other mid-17th-century teenage undesirables. Half-starved escapees from bad harvests. & unemployment. Who have received their century's message of rational materialism. & refuse to be fed on oldfashioned paternalistic promises of posthumous Paradise. & believe that Heaven & Hell are states of mind, not places. & know that the rich have inherited the earth. & that the term 'the people' does not include the poor. (Or women.) & are applying their century's rational materialist theory by picking pockets & mugging marketing matrons & burglarizing burghers' houses.

Singing while they work:

> 'The law locks up the man or woman
> That steals the goose from off the common;
> But leaves the greater villain loose
> Who steals the common from the goose.'

& other equally subversive mid-17th-century ditties. While waiting to be picked up. & shipped off to the new world. To a new England. A new York. That will be more tolerant than the old. Where everything will be electric with progress, down to the chairs.

Where they can continue to practice rationalized materialism with the encouragement of the law they left behind.

Where Honor can become a New-World prostitute. & maybe start a collection of scalps & shrunken heads & pilgrims' bones, after she makes her first fatherless million.

& Charity can become a nun. & subsequent New-World saint, after she converts the Red Indians to the crucial truths of Christianity.

Maybe she'll also learn Spanish, & be enshrined in Vera Cruz . . .

He finds himself yelling at the twins for sneaking out on Bô Hookker. For not helping him save the man. Who is a purer man than his resentful puritan executioners.

An unusually forgiving husband. A loving father, even if he hadn't kissed them very often.

B. H. has certainly been a better man than *he* has been, up to his 45th birthday. Which B. H. well deserves to wake up to. In his own   if wifeless   mid-17th-century bed above the print shop.

A better-looking man, too. Much trimmer around the middle. In spite   or perhaps because   of 11 years of servants' food.

His eyes look clear. Well-lashed & pouchless.

(As do those of most of the wife-beaters. & of most of the wives.

With a few cross-eyed exceptions most mid-17th-century eyes look   & seem to see   better than most late-20th-century eyes.

Perhaps over 3 centuries of compulsory reading   one third of it by artificial light   has resulted not in enlightenment so much as in weakened vision. A hereditary need to wear glasses.

Perhaps compulsory literacy is a sin against the species.

A sin which had not yet become organic, during the 17th century. When education was still a privilege rather than law-enforced eye strain. & clear-eyed scholars studied to make their own demanding grades.

Perhaps mass media have blocked the flow of life. & books have become enlightening mainly to their authors.

Who have gone blind in the process of writing them by artificial light. Their sight dimming with increasing enlightenment. Oedipal wrecks who depend on tax-deductible donations to P.O. Box 20-20 for their survival.)

Perhaps the clear-eyed Beaufort Hookker learned justice &

tolerance from the pamphlets he wrote. (& didn't talk away to an audience of female listeners in preparation for bed.)

Unlike some, the clear-eyed Beaufort Hookker wrote first, & set his type. & seduced later. He didn't mistake lust for love. He was *not* an inferior man.

He was a real writer.

& a political figure.

He was a sincerely committed citizen who fought 17th-century monopolies with the quixotic courage of a latter-day folder/stapler/mutilator of computerized holy writs. & he is about to be made into a martyr by a bunch of wife-beaters.

How can the twins let a man be hanged for having a bit of a roving eye! Where is *their* tolerance? *Their* sense of justice? Don't they care about what is happening in Ireland? Still! 325 years later!

Which might not be happening if Bô Hookker had been allowed to live out his historically predestined life!

Hadn't they wanted to change the course of history? At least the saintly half of them. & unmake the mistakes of the past? Why are they now so callous? Why don't they crawl right back through the circling forest of impatient female legs, & *do* something! They're right down there! Ubiquity has its obligations!

But the twins have become timelessly agelessly wise. They shake their reddish heads. & smile serenely. & stick fresh joints between their knowing Irish lips.

They're still his parents; only wiser.

"It's the martyr who makes history. Executioners merely execute," his saintly father says to him. Does he think Christianity could have snowballed without the Crucifixion?

"Punishment alleviates the torture of guilt by transferring the pain from within to without," sighs his mother. & frowns patiently when he protests that Bô Hookker hasn't done anything to feel guilty about.

Why won't they help him save an innocent man!

"Good intentions sometimes have worse results than bad intentions," his father explains with a smile.

"Inertia is sometimes the more effective course of action," echoes his mother.

"Correct the perspective, & the illusion disappears," they chorus. Stinging his eyes with the acid smoke from their joints.

& they illustrate their words of wisdom with slides which they project for him onto their private screen above the pilot seat.

He watches the mickey-mouse watch which had rebounded to his left hand materialize in the more vigorous abler left hand of the about-to-be-hanged Bô Hookker. The hand with which the master-printer & leveller used to set his type. & write his pamphlets.

At the moment it is clenched into a fist. & aimed at the upturned nose of one of the 5 retaliating wife-beaters who is inviting him to say a canonical prayer before they kick a milking stool out from under his feet.

The upturned nose remains unpunched. Bô Hookker retrieves his fist. Brings it up to his eyes. Opens it. Peers at the glistening ticking object in his palm.

He can see it clearly in the light of the moon. It is a chronometer. But unlike any he has seen. He wonders who slipped it into his hand.

He takes it to mean that his time is up.

& that his manhood is being likened unflatteringly to the caricature of an aggressive mouse.

For an instant he wishes that he had been born a woman. His wife. Any one of his 7 daughters. His fat prosperous sister, even. Any woman. That he could live happily hidden behind the backs of men. Protected first by a good father, & later by a good husband. Modest by nature. Exempt from politics. Without the temptation of arrogance or ambition.

(Which he would not wish if he could forsee the pending fulfillment: the atrophied body of a clammy little girl.)

(He doesn't realize how careful one must be about one's wishes, however fleeting. How specific, lest the fulfillment leave one worse off than before.

He can't imagine being worse off than he is. Nor does he obviously anticipate fulfillment of his wish. From where he's standing   atop a shaky milking stool, with a noose around his neck   a woman's life looks enviable. He'd rather dance around his cherry tree than dangle from it.)

Why are they so eager to see him hang.

He can't believe that anyone in York seriously believes that he's a papist. Do they really suspect him of murdering his wife?

He must have made more enemies than he thought. Even of women. Even of the women he had always thought rather fancied him.

Who had perhaps not fancied *him,* but his fancy for them. & had mistaken his normal male desire for a deeper sentiment.

(Which is still reserved for his run-away wife. Who had perhaps felt insulted by his possessiveness.

With whom his sister had never linked arms before. His sister is congratulating his wife on her impending widowhood.)

Perhaps he had insulted the women who fancied him by not insisting when they refused his advances.

Unless they hadn't fancied him at all. & it had all been his arrogant male illusion.

He obviously doesn't know women. Knows women only from the outside in.

They've probably despised him all along.

Perhaps even his daughters despise him. Except Patty, he hopes.

Perhaps they can't wait for him to die, so they can be free

to follow in their mother's footsteps, & run off to wherever they please. He's a fool to worry about what will become of them   more than about what will become of him   after he dies.

He looks questioningly down at Leonora at the foot of the tree. Perhaps Leonora has painted the disagreeable mouse on the ominous chronometer. He has often had the feeling that Leonora resents him. & blames him for their mother's leaving.
Perhaps all his daughters blame him for it. Except Patty, who blames their mother.

Leonora's face is a puzzled blank as he dangles the object in front of her eyes.
Someone slaps it out of his hand. It drops to the still frozen NE English March ground. & is probably broken.
Several wife-beaters get down on their hands & knees & grope for it. Nobody is paying attention to him on top of the milking stool.
It occurs to him that whoever slipped the thing into his hand may conceivably be a friend. Perhaps the only friend he has in all of York. & that he must use the momentary distraction which the helpful friend intended to attempt an escape.
He is able to wriggle his head out of the noose. Which gives a little as he pulls at it with both hands. & practically skins his cheeks. He has always been a little vain about his fair delicate skin.
He slides off the stool, & breaks his right ankle.
The wife-beaters straighten up. & scowl at him, lying noose-less on the ground, holding his foot.
One of them dangles the objectionable object in front of his eyes. Back & forth. Back & forth. Like a pendulum.
It is still ticking.

It occurs to him that he, too, will swing like a pendulum in the nightwind, after they string him up again. As they inescapably will. That his body will clock the time which for him   has stopped.

The wives & daughters have come closer. They are forming an ever tighter circle around him. Towering above him   ominously tall   their eyes following the ticking swinging object.
On which several women clearly discern the ink-black picture of the devil.
In whom most of their mid-17th-century husbands &/or fathers have become too enlightened to believe.
Still . . . why take chances.
They swarm to his tool shed & find his ax. They chop down the cherry tree & burn the liar alive. Painfully slowly, on the green-smoking wood.
Which the wives & daughters fan with their skirts as they dance around him. Chanting:

>   Devil devil burning bright
>   In the orchard of the night
>   His immoral hand & eye
>   Still mime his spiteful heresy . . .

In psychic parody of William Blake, whose birth is still 109 years away.

Who would certainly be a happier reincarnation   for Beaufort Hookker   for all concerned   than the unfortunate, fortunately short-lived little girl.
But apparently undeserved.

The wives & daughters have switched to a livelier rhythm, & are chanting:

> Fry, fry, kiss the devil goodbye
> Burn the leveller on his level though the wood isn't dry
> Pale blue flames lick his blistering lies
> Singing this'll be the day that he dies . . .

Meanwhile, back in the plane, he is grateful to the twins for preventing him from making matters worse for Beaufort Hookker. Whose fate can perhaps be more effectively corrected at an earlier stage.

He is glad to see the man grow younger. A handsome trim 37. Sitting in his print shop, surrounded by his 7 daughters. Who are helping him set an anti-monopoly pamphlet, entitled: Englands Complaint to Jesus Christ against the Bishops Canons.
 Little Patty who is only 3½ is putting in a comma, with her tiny fingers.
 2 women have walked in. Both thick-ankled & wide-mouthed. Visibly mother & daughter. Decidedly not his type. But they seem to be Bô Hookker's type. Unless Bô Hookker tells every woman who walks into his shop how lonely it feels to be without a wife. That his wife has walked out on him & on his 7 young daughters inexplicably. As though *she* were the husband, & *he* the wife. & mother. For no good reason he can think of. He has never beaten her. Or blamed her for bearing him only daughters. He's always loved her well.
 He always loves well when he loves.
 Leonora nudges Kate.
 Who nudges Deborah. Who shrugs.
 Carey stands up, deliberately blocking the 2 women from little Patty's view.

The twins giggle. & make moon-eyes at each other. They're much too aware for 2 little girls of not quite 5.

Bô Hookker at 35, sitting at one small end of his long dining table of polished cherry wood. Presiding over his 7 motherless daughters. Who are aligned along the 2 long sides of the table in blatant disregard of chronological order. In order of paternal preference.

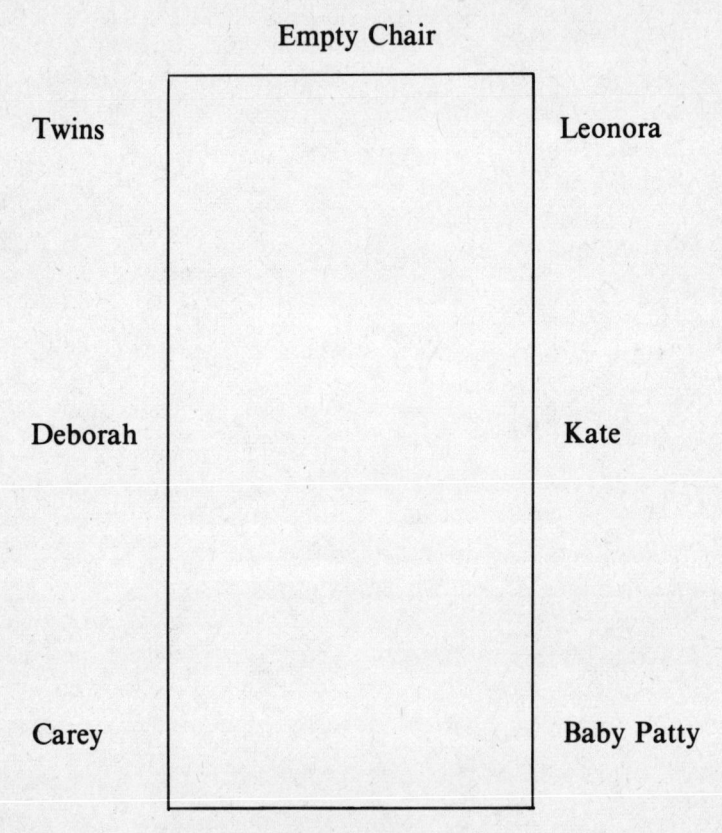

```
                    Empty Chair
         ┌─────────────────────────────┐
 Twins   │                             │   Leonora
         │                             │
         │                             │
         │                             │
 Deborah │                             │   Kate
         │                             │
         │                             │
         │                             │
 Carey   │                             │   Baby Patty
         └─────────────────────────────┘
                    Bô Hookker
```

Baby Patty on his right, in a high chair, opposite Carey on his left.
Then Kate opposite Deborah.
& last Leonora opposite the 3-year-old twins.

He has just received his new drinking glasses. & is toasting the empty chair at the other small end of the table across from him   with an empty plate & new drinking glass set in front of it. Where his freckle-faced Irish witch-wife used to sit   when the children left her the time to sit down with him & eat the food she had cooked. Before she walked out on them all a year ago to the day.

For a full year Bồ Hookker has kept his wife's place lovingly set at the dinner table, expecting her to walk back in as unexpectedly as she walked out.

She is about to do just that.

Running backward into the dining room after the door flies open as though pushed by a storm. Plopping down the kitten she'd snatched up a year before. Discarding the mantle she'd thrust about her shoulders with a gesture of finality worthy of classical Greek drama.

Played backwards, tragedy looks ridiculous. It relies on chronological sequence for its effect.

He had been curious to see if the much-regretted Mrs. Bồ Hookker looked in any way like his own Irish concert-harpist wife Maureen. She does not. If anything she reminds him of Ilona, freckles & reddish hair nothwithstanding.

She also sounds like Ilona. Telling Beaufort Hookker that she's tired of playing backdrop to a protesting Protestant who levels eyes with the wives & daughters of the saps who listen to him preach his home-made justice & tolerance. A pseudo-saint who goes around the house pinching the maids' bottoms which he has stopped beating.

Who thinks that whatever he feels like doing   & does   is always good. Best for all concerned. Noble. A blessing for the Commonwealth. The salvation of Ireland. & that if she maybe doesn't like it at first, she'll soon grow to like it. As soon as she comes to her senses.

If he'd at least express a doubt from time to time. If he'd at least say that he'd do better if he knew better. Instead of expecting applause from his victims.

Has he ever paused to ask himself, if not her: she asks if it has been good for her to bear 7 daughters 2 of them twins in not quite 10 years?

Perhaps she doesn't enjoy conceiving. & being pregnant practically every summer. & giving milk like a cow. & thinking in baby talk for the most intelligent years of her life.

Has it ever occurred to him that she might perhaps not *like* children? That perhaps not all women wanted to be mothers!

It has occurred to him that there are hookers & Hookkers: smiles her hooked sap of a husband. Who is running greedy fingers through her thick rust-red hair.

Instead of grabbing her by it & beating her black & blue in front of their 7 round-eyed daughters as is his enviable early-to-mid-17th-century privilege. As yet uncurtailed by law. As yet unrestricted to the hours between 5 a.m. & 9 p.m.

It makes him lose interest in Beaufort Hookker. Why waste his scanty imagination trying to correct the fate of a man who marries a commendable one-night stand, & spends the remainder of his grass-widowed life missing her. Baying over her loss until his neighbors put a rope around his neck to shut him up.

It even somewhat revises his opinion of the wife-beating executioners.

Unfairly: according to the suddenly sympathetic twins. Who beg him to reconsider. How can he dismiss a man for his taste in women. "Men who make history don't necessarily have model home lives," they assure him.

They urge him to take a second look. Not at Mrs. Hookker, since Mrs. Hookker turns him off. But at the 7 arbitrarily aligned dining daughters. Perhaps that's where he'll find the resemblance he's been looking for.

Obviously he doesn't see what they see. Unless they're putting him on. What possible resemblance can there be between the remote glass beauty of a Deborah, & his droopy-winged little harpist-wife.

Whom he wouldn't have married if she'd been beautiful: he assures the twins.
His wife is better-looking than he is talented. & far more talented than he is good-looking: *they* assure *him*.
How do *they* know what his wife looks like? He wishes he carried a photograph of her in his wallet, to show to them.
They have seen her picture. On the poster in the glass cage outside the concert hall. A gigantic blow-up of her talented face.
Has he forgotten that his wife has become recognized? Like his teenage baby sister. Unlike him. She is well on her way to fame.
No wonder she walked out on him if he made her feel ugly all the time.
He did *not* make her feel ugly. He has just told them: he *prefers* homely women.
He challenges them to find a single beauty among his many girlfriends. (Except for their unanimously well-shaped legs. He's always had a thing about legs.)
Patricia is too tall to be considered beautiful. She's altogether too large.
He has made a point of staying away from beautiful women. His mother has been a warning to him.
He worked hard to free himself from his mother's influence: he tells the twins. He was close to 30, when it finally dawned on him that not all her truths were true.

That's the first thing he tells any new girlfriend: Start doubting your mother's truths. He has liberated quite a number of them, in that way . . .

They shrug. & smile pityingly. & blow smoke rings into his eyes.

His mother was an exception: they inform him. Most beautiful women are less demanding & truer than ugly ones. Who are forever on the lookout for reassurance.

Who are ugly only because they lack the imagination to correct the impression they make. Ugliness is only skin deep . . .

"Proportion is the secret of beauty," the twins declare, in sudden plastic-surgeons' voices. Pulling out tape measures. & pointing them at Deborah's slightly lower forehead & slightly rounder chin & slightly thinner nose.

They propose to demonstrate what they mean by redoing his face for him.

They promise they'll make him look beautiful, without changing the basic structure of his chubby features. Right then & there, while he watches in the magnifying mirror over the pilot seat.

"Any special Greek god you'd like to look like?" they inquire, smoothing transparent rubber gloves over their jittery grass-stained fingers. Swearing Hippocratic oaths at each other.

He doesn't want to look beautiful. He wants to look handsome. Where is their sense of sexual propriety?

They giggle uncontrollably. & point blunt scalpels at his crotch. Does he want them to operate on his male chauvinism?

They invite him to sit in the pilot seat. Cross-legged, for better exposure. He needn't be afraid. They're a team of painless dentists. He won't feel a thing.

INTER - MISSION

The curtain is of such fullness
that the polestars can be seen at noon.

BEFORE	AFTER
A chubbily youthful professional dilettante. Compulsorily literate eyes with nascent pouches seductively concealed behind Mod/Mad.-Ave. shades from the Mod/Mad.-Ave. opticians who change your image in an hour.	No Mod/Mad.-Ave. shades & . . . No . . . O no . . . O no . . . O no . . .

(The mere thought of
contact lenses—of a
foreign body in his body
 . . . in his eyes! . . .
irritates his cornea.)

The twins must have gone through with at least one of their proffered operations. Only the first one, he hopes. Which is bad enough. The sad double-chinned face that is frowning at him out of the magnifying mirror is hardly a recommendation for their surgical skills. Even if he didn't feel a thing. Which he didn't.

Unless they maliciously intended to make him look lbs. heavier & years older. In keeping with their peculiar sense of humor. More like a temporarily shadeless Mad. Ave. ad. exec. on a steady Martini diet than a professionally frugal prof. of Eng. Lit. / writer who is taking notes on life. A sad ungodly Roman rather than the proposed Greek god.

Whom he failed to choose.

& they have chosen one for him. From the rogues' gallery of the Greco-Roman underworld. A pig-eyed Pluto-Vulcanus. To teach him to make up his mind the next time he's given the chance of a choice.

To play a practical joke on his youthfulness of which he's always been a little proud. To make him realize that chubby immaturity is more than skin deep.

He wishes they'd left well enough alone. & had refrained

from tampering with his face. Even if they think that they own it, since he picked them to be his parents.

He realizes that his skull is nothing but the convex replica of his mother's womb. Still, that does not entitle her to a lifetime concession on it, inside as well as outside.

& what have they done to his hair!

Nothing! they protest, their voices high-pitched with indignation.
(Unless he is hearing the echo of his own voice, & they have also gone through with the second   equally successful operation.)
They have done nothing! Except save his thankless life, after he tried to dive from the cockpit when they started to pull down his pants.
They're saints   or masochists   to keep bothering with him in exchange for nothing but ingratitude. What makes him think that parents owe life-long credit to their son!
They wish he'd straighten out.
& up. They're tired of holding on to his legs   each to one leg   while he's hanging head-down over ancient Rome, getting a bird's-eye close-up of part of the ancient history he almost majored in.
The sad fat face he's been looking at is not his magnified mirror image. Not his current magnified mirror image, at any rate. It belongs to a sad stout   & bald   early-IV-century Roman. A gouty patrician & high priest by the name of Belfortis Hamus.

(The following era is dedicated to my good friend Armand Handfus. My oldest friend in NYC. *Bel* homme *fort* intelligent; & désarmant . . .)

Belfortis Hamus is sitting on a black marble bench across from the sundial in his garden behind his villa, exposing painfully swollen feet & thumbs to the early afternoon sunshine of the Roman spring of CCCIII. Contemplating a life-size bronze bust of himself. A present from his only   late son Belfortis Hamus Verus for his XLV birthday. March XXIV, CCCIII.

Which is also the day on which his only son, Belfortis Hamus Verus, ceased to live.

Shortly after noon. At the still promising age of XXIV.

His XLI-year-old wife Patricina who supervised the sculpting & casting of the bust while committing sodomy with the sculptor   a red-bearded thin slave, brought back from Britain a year before, as a present for his XLIV birthday by their only late son B. H. V. (of whose death his wife Patricina is as yet unaware)   has had the bust placed in the center of the sundial. As a tribute to the sculpting slave more than to the model master.

It replaces the shaft that normally casts the shadow of time, & is much less precise. Belfortis Hamus has difficulty deciding whether it is shortly after I or close to II o'clock.

Man   he thinks   has little control over the shadow he casts. It is the shadow, not the man, that measures man's progress in time.

He will have the shaft restored: he decides, with apologies to his bust.

Which he will have moved to another   less conspicuous   location. Where the ambiguous inscription *EGO SUM QUI SUM* on the pedestal, directly under the gleaming   flatteringly trimmer   bronze chest will be lost in a thicket of sprouting mimosa. Hidden from casually reading visitors who might recognize *I am who am . . . I am that I am . . .* as a quotation from the long-haired founder of the

Christian religion. & wonder what a long-haired Christian quotation might be doing in the garden of a Roman high priest . . . Directly under the high priest's very own bronze heart. From the bottom of . . . *ab imo pectore* . . .

Which might have stimulated casually interesting conversations about comparative religions . . . about the function of religion in different societies . . . which often seem to miss the point & sacrifice the content to the cult . . . V or VI years ago. When the peasant emperor Diocletian   a freedman's son; who should have been a gardener, not an emperor   was still tolerating Christians. Permitting them to infiltrate even the higher branches of his low-brow government. The army, even. Until it belatedly occurred to the imperial peasant brain that non-violence & brotherly love don't wage successful colonial wars.

Even a year ago such a conversation might still have been possible. When the gardener was just beginning to weed Christians out of the higher echelons of his armies.

When friends had still been possible. Without the constant fear that one of them might turn *delatore*. & level a charge of Christian sympathies against his host. Whose well-kept house & garden   & art work   & well-fed slaves   he has envied for years. Without being in a position to acquire parts thereof as a reward for betraying a trusting friend's hospitality.

Belfortis Hamus wishes that he could go back in time. To a time when he had still enjoyed having a birthday.

When each birthday had been an occasion not only to celebrate   with his dear Patricina & their beloved only son B. H. V.   but also to start thinking afresh.

When thinking had still been permitted.

When he had sat in his garden on a mellow evening   as yet goutless   in the company of trusted/trusting friends, casually gathered around the sundial. Revising prejudices. Thoughts about life.

About time. Which man has falsified, in the process of measuring it. Upon which man has committed the crime of chronology. Deriving a false security from the shadow's repetitive circle game. Mistaking continuity for growth . . .

Friendly words, flowing with the warm ease of the good Hamus wine. A true gift of the gods.

. . . Of God! smiles his son. Who never misses an opportunity to proselytize.

. . . Why pray to dozens of gods when you can pray to all of them in one? he asks. His earnest face aglow between loose shoulder-long hair, after the second cup. Perhaps a third. Religious fervor has not quenched his son's congenital thirst for wine.

Which so happens to have been the favorite beverage of the long-haired founder of the Christian religion. The one who was who was. Whom his son has been trying to emulate. The alleged son of the one & only God of the Christians. Who had, however, respected & obeyed *his* father.

. . . The Christian God incorporates & supersedes all other gods. Roman gods. Greek gods. Phoenician gods. Even the gods of the barbarians. Primitive limited oldfashioned materialistic deities. Which are expressions of man's subconscious recognition that God exists. A recognition which the Divine Son has pulled up from the subconscious into man's consciousness . . .: his son informs a politely astonished audience, friends of his father, high priest of Rome.

The mellow garden air is thick with his sincerity.

. . . The symbols differ from religion to religion: the proselytizer continues. From country to country. But the instinctive understanding behind the symbols is groping toward the same universal God-conscious one-ness . . .

. . . Which is why all men are brothers . . .

... Who must therefore stop fighting & enslaving each other. & unite in worship of their sole Creator ...

It is unsolicited opinions such as these that prompted the peasant emperor to use violence against non-violence, thinks Belfortis Hamus. Massaging his hurting thumbs. Wishing that he'd never had a son.

For whom he & his dear as yet faithful Patricina had ardently wished, at the beginning of their marriage.
Whom they had loved a little more each day as they watched him grow. Growing more intelligent than either of his parents. Who had not ceased being impressed with the scope & depth of their growing son's thoughts. Which neither parent could recall having thought much less expressed when they had been VIII & XI & XII years old.
When *they* had not asked *their* parents at age VIII if the liar from Crete who says that he's a liar is telling the truth? & if he's telling the truth, how can he be a liar? Or can the truth also be a lie?
When they had not lain awake all night at age XIII thinking about illusion. After learning about the Great Alexander's interest in the religions of the East. & had not asked *their* father in the morning: 'Supposing the world really is illusion. Then man as part of the world must be part of the illusion. How can an illusion know that it is illusion?'
To which Belfortis Hamus had found no answer to give his XIII-year-old son.
Who was a genius, he had thought. Smiling. Under the happy illusion that having a genius for a son would bring fulfillment to the parents. Especially to the father. Whose latent potentials the genius son was realizing.
(A woman automatically realized *her* potential in motherhood: he had thought.)
A genius son could not but increase the fame & fortune of the noble name of Hamus. Which did after all mean 'hook'.

An ingenious hook with which to catch the golden fish of glory.

Perhaps he & his dear Patricina would one day experience the supreme satisfaction of having an emperor for a son. A well-born enlightened emperor whose judicious reign would unite the world under Roman rule.

Who would be deified during his lifetime.

Together with his parents. To whom he would erect statues all over his empire, in loving gratitude for having raised him. For having made him what he is.

The genius son had soon stopped asking questions of his father.

Who had soon stopped smiling.

Whose permission the genius son neglected to ask at age XIX when he volunteered to lead one of the peasant emperor's campaigns against Britain. Jeopardizing the fulfillment of his promising brilliance. Torturing his anguished parents with the constant fear of losing him while he conquered colonies for the peasant emperor's glorification.

Nor would the genius son listen at age XXIV when his father pleaded with him to remember his noble birth. Which was after all an obligation. Toward others as well as toward himself. & not to debase the noble name of Hamus by walking around on naked soles. Claiming that the high patrician *sandalium* was unnatural to the foot. & looked ridiculous, like everything that was unnatural. & inhibited walking.

Which was true, perhaps.

But so was the ancient advice never to ignore the possibility of inhibition where the moods of one's own heart were concerned. Because inhibition was the basis of human freedom.

Besides, the effort of walking kept the higher-born mindful of their station.

Which was less unnatural than a patrician's son's willful lowering himself to the slave level. Squatting on naked heels in the slaves' quarters, discussing religious philosophies as though they were his equals.

Which the slaves knew that they were not. But feigned to be, to please their young master. Slavishly feigning conversion to the Christian God, while they shrugged & snickered behind his back. & worked less well. & less. & began losing respect. Not only for him but for his parents as well. Beginning to judge their masters. Which was always the beginning of disobedience & social unrest.

Could he not think of his dear mother's safety, at least, if he could not respect his father's position as Roman high priest, & stop walking barefoot & loose-haired through the streets of Rome, talking universal love & brotherhood to the rabble. Inviting ridicule & stones & spit in the face in reply to his childish, childishly arrogant mission to put an end to pain & fear. Provoking the violence he said he wanted to abolish.

Transferring the fear & the pain not to mention embarrassment, the basic social emotion onto his pleading father. Whom he said he loved. & respected. But whom he said he could not help. Who was able to help himself. Whereas his mission was to help the helpless.

& to save his soul.

What selfishness, this Christian preoccupation with the salvation of one's soul, thinks Belfortis Hamus. Wishing that he'd had an only daughter instead of an only son.

A reassuringly average only daughter. Neither remarkably beautiful nor remarkably intelligent. Who if married might have presented him with a grandson for his XLV birthday, rather than with a flatteringly trimmer bronze replica of his upper parts.

Or perhaps his daughter would have become a Vestal. Who would have added to her pontifex father's prestige. & security.

& might have saved the life of an unfortunate patrician's proselytizing son who happened to cross her redeeming path on his way to the forum. Where he will burn alive rather than listen to his father's pleas.

A moderately handsome XXIV-year-old daughter who   married or not   might compete with her mother for the artful attentions of the slave from Britain. & win out, on the strength of her comparative youth. Which most slaves prefer to maturity. It takes freedom to appreciate the flowers of decay. The lowly don't know how to be decadent. They have no position to fall from . . .

Although his wife's slumming with the slave is the least of his concerns at the moment.

It is certainly preferable to her previous attempts to seduce their only son, after his return from the campaign in Britain. When she wanted their only son to give her a practical demonstration of the universal love he had come home preaching. From which she saw no reason to be excluded.

Show me: she kept nagging: Show me. If you don't *show* love, you don't love . . .

To which their only son kept replying   always with the same, slightly exasperating patient smile: That he *was* showing her love. Filial love. & respect. Not because he was afraid of committing incest. Which was one of the few still forbidden fruit, in sinful polytheistic Rome. Nor because he thought that she was too old to be desirable. But she was not only his mother, but also his father's wife. & his new religion forbade him to covet another man's wife.

Besides, the love of his God was not the decaying love of the flesh. But the immutable love of the soul.

He loved all of mankind. According to age as fathers or mothers, brothers or sisters, sons or daughters . . .

Which had exasperated his poor dear Patricina. & had driven her to drinking a whole *congius* (0.8 U.S. gallon) of the good Hamus wine a night. Twice as much as before their only son's return from Britain. When she had drunk half a *congius,* to keep herself from worrying about their absent only son.

Of whose death she will have to be made aware sooner or later. By no one but himself. If it weren't for his poor dear Patricina, Belfortis Hamus would go back inside his villa & lie down next to his late only son B. H. V., & open his veins.

He dearly loves the foolish woman. Whom he still sees as the XVI-year-old he had married.
Whose appetite for sex used to exhaust him. After baffling him. After filling him with newly-married pride. She'd do better, if she knew better. & is obviously going through the embarrassing age women go through, on the picket fence of XL.
As do men. Although less embarrassingly, society being in league with procreation.
He doesn't blame his Patricina for having recourse to the slave. His feet & thumbs hurt much too much to keep her occupied.
But he will feign indignation to justify the moving & eventual destruction of the bust. Which he would destroy with his own painful hands right then & there, if he could. If freshly cast bronze were as accommodating as XXIV-year-old wine-drugged flesh.
He will have the Britain melt down the bust. & fashion a bust of their son instead. With the unambiguous inscription *DULCE ET DECORUM EST PRO PATRIA MORI* across the pedestal. To honor the memory of their late & only son B. H. V.
Under the continued supervision of his dear insatiable wife.

Whom he will try to acquaint gently, gradually, with the fatal news.

Their only son has been cured of his Christian folly & has returned to Britain at the emperor's urgent request: he will tell her, blending fiction with facts. Later . . . after she has started drinking. . . . Before he tells her that their only son has died a hero's patriotic death . . .

Which had almost become a fact, a couple of years before. In the early spring of CCC. When their only son was holding an outpost near Eboracum (York), NE Britain. When a sentinel sighted the approach of barbarian hordes that far outnumbered the Romans. There had been no hope of survival.

But then one of his son's men a soldier from Judea had gone down on his knees & started praying. To the Christian God. The one who is who is. & soon after, a heavy snow had begun to fall. Which happens occasionally, although rarely, in the early springs of barbaric NE Britain.

The snow had built a high white wall around the outpost. Which had concealed his son & his son's men from the approaching hordes, until the bulk of the Roman army arrived & defeated the enemy.

In the spring of CCCII their son had returned to Rome, just in time for his father's XLIV birthday. With V barbarian slaves as a birthday gift.

Which he later asked to take back. When his religious madness increased, & he tried to convert the V barbarians to the God that had saved him. (& enslaved *them*.) Trying to persuade his father to give them their freedom & let them return to Britain & proselytize.

Instead of accepting the governorship of Britain & returning to Eboracum (York), NE Britain, his unfathomable son had turned in his victorious sword. & sworn never to kill another man as long as he lived. Not even in self-defense. To stay in Rome & devote his saved life to spreading the word of the foreign Christian God.

Which would have been well & good   (only a trifle humiliating, socially. Christianity was after all a lower-class religion. Still, having their son safely home would have made his parents happy.)   if the young genius had bothered keeping abreast of the peasant emperor's politics. Or if he had at least listened to his father & kept his soul-saving opinions to himself.

If he had not relied on his father to step in before it was too late. & save him from a dishonorable death   by public torture, in the forum   to which he exposed himself a little more each day, on his bare-foot loose-haired rounds.

Intentionally, perhaps.

Perhaps his son had hoped to provoke public dishonor without consideration for his parents' feelings or position   in ultimate emulation of the loose-haired founder of the Christian religion. Whom his followers had deified, allegedly, after he had allegedly been tortured to death in public, in the company of II thieves.

Perhaps his son had hoped that he, too, would be deified. Blatantly contradicting his vociferous belief in an only God. Which had already been sufficiently contradicted by that only God's deified alleged only son.

One only-father-god plus one only-son-god made II gods, in Belfortis Hamus' ledger. He was after all not unacquainted with the needle points of religions. He was after all high priest of Rome.

The Son is the Father made flesh. The same essence, but not the same substance: smiles his exasperating son. Who had been the better dialectitian since age XIII.

The Christian God had not saved the Roman high priest's

only son a second time, on his father's XLV birthday, shortly after noon. In spite of the omnipresence the son claimed his god possessed.

Perhaps the Christian God agreed with the father rather than with the son.

Who had done nothing to defend his still promising XXIV-year-old life.

Who had encouraged his hesitant father in a moment of semi-consciousness; under the spell of the heavily drugged wine to complete what he had begun.

Thanking his incredulous father for assisting him at both ends of life. For taking his death into his helpful hands, like a midwife. Permitting his soul to ascend straight to Heaven. & sit at the feet of his God.

To be returned to earth at a later . . . better . . . more enlightened . . . more tolerant time in history. In the body of a free Britain. A poet-prophet by the name of Gulielmus Blake.

Unless his son's God is a vengeful god. & is waiting for the propitious moment, omnipresent in the garden, biding his time in the form of a bush or a bird.

An ancient Roman pigeon has inaugurated Belfortis Hamus' new bronze bust. A white chalky streak birthmarks the left side of the firmer bronze face.

At present it is picking ancient Roman lice out from under its left wing pit. In an instant it will fly away. Backward, in rhythm with the shadow which the bust is casting onto the perimeter of the sundial. & which is slowly sliding from early afternoon back toward noon. When Belfortis Hamus Verus was still alive.

The twins are hanging over the cockpit on either side of him, twittering with excitement. Urging him to compare the bust to the model. & the model to the bust.

Does he notice how the bust's chin is more heroic. How much nobler the bronze brow. & there's a lot more determination in the bronze cheeks & the trimmer bronze chest. & yet. & yet! The basic structure has not been changed. What did they tell him about proportion being the secret of beauty! That sculptor-slave from Britain would have made a first-rate plastic surgeon.

It is the less saintly half of them   the horror-filming sister; his unapplauded star-mother   who drops the mickey-mouse watch at Belfortis Hamus' painful feet, in pathetically oversized black sandals on high patrician cork soles. Interrupting the painful feet's patrician backward shuffle toward the villa. Toward the cool dark room in which Belfortis Hamus Verus lies as though asleep.

The stout bald man painfully puffs down & picks the object up.

Which must be some kind of bug, he thinks, listening to the nervous heartbeat. Which reminds him of the metallic sound of crickets. A foreign type of louse or bed bug which a rarely washing soldier has brought back from the colonies. Where these creatures grow larger than in Rome. With strange black markings on their grey backs that vaguely resemble script . . . & a mouse . . .

Ridiculus mus: mutters Belfortis Hamus. & throws the bug into the mimosa bushes. Distractedly hoping that he has not thrown a foreign garden pest into the tender young leaves. But he has more important things to think about. He has just strangled his only son. With his own painful hands. Which feel more painful than before. Which he stands contemplating under the portal of his villa.

Enraging both twins. Who unleash a hailstorm of mickey-mouse watches on the bald contemplative head. Aiming extra-painful pellets at the swollen thumbs. At the bulky crimson-glistening toes in the pathetic sandals. Into the surprised face that looks up with sudden blinded faith at the manifestation of the omnipresent vengeful Christian God. & into the gasping quivering mouth. Which emits a choking scream.

Meanwhile, inside the villa, in one of the cool dark rooms, Belfortis Hamus Verus is coming back to life. Without his father's helpful hands around his throat. Which he clasps with both hands. Swearing the solemn oath never   never   to drink so much wine again. Not even on his father's birthdays.
He feels decidedly hung over. Which is unworthy of a follower of the Son of God. Harmful to the God-consciousness he is striving to evolve. Too much wine ferments the brain . . .
Which is shaped like a walnut, he thinks, smiling faintly. Thinking of II shelled walnut halves swimming in a cup of wine.
From the bottom of his subconscious rises a sunset-red float of a vision. In which he dies   half in his sleep   strangled by his own father's gouty hands. & becomes transparent light. & ascends to Heaven. & sits at the feet of God for several hundreds of years. Which feel shorter than a day.
& is returned to earth. & lives in the far distant future, as a rusty-maned Britain named Gulielmus Somebody or Other. A stocky merchant's son with a large head. & large luminous eyes. A poet who takes dictation from God. & leads the

outwardly uneventful life of a prophet who rises & falls with his mission.

In the company of a softly faithful wife.

Belfortis Hamus Verus tries to interpret his vision. Which is perhaps a warning from his God. Who does perhaps not approve of the way in which he has been spreading His Divine Word.

Who agrees with his father, perhaps. & is urging him to obey his father. To be silent & inconspicuous. To marry a softly faithful wife   (who may be hard to find, in sinful polytheistic Rome)   & lead an outwardly uneventful life, taking quiet notes on life until the time is ripe to speak out.

He jumps at his father's scream from the garden. & feels a choking pain in his throat. Which he clutches as he runs out.

& collides with the sculptor-slave from Britain who comes rushing from his mother's apartments. Followed by his mother, who is swaying on her high white sandals, clutching a cup of wine.

The entire Hamus household is rushing out into the unusual hailstorm.

Which some take to be a swarm of unusual foreign insects. Subversively smuggled in from the colonies, where vermin & weeds grow larger than in Rome.

Which all interpret as a manifestation of divine wrath, whether of one God or of several Gods.

Hands raised to shield their heads, crunching the unusual pellets or insects under bare or sandaled feet, monotheists & polytheists perform a grotesquely stylized heron's dance around their master.

Who has sunken to his knees, rasping: The vengeful god. The omnipresent vengeful god . . .

& dies of a heart attack   on his XLV birthday; at the precise moment of noon (which his new bronze bust is marking with an imprecise shadow that spreads from XI:L to XII:X on the perimeter of the sundial)   at the sight of his son who has rushed to his side & is trying to lift him up.

The son's long loose hair falls like a curtain over the father's fear-frozen face.

> (End of special dedication
> to Armand Handfus.)

Acta est fabula! shout the twins, applauding crazily.
They're delirious. The mickey-mouse watches have finally fulfilled their purpose. A dual purpose. The saintly brother has saved the good son, the true Belfortis Hamus (Verus), & has punished the murderous father.
Whom he has saved from being a murderer by saving the son.
& whom he has moveover converted to Christianity. Somewhat brutally perhaps, but nonetheless.
& his not-so-saintly more realistic sister has filmed the most incredible documentary the most sensational piece of cine-verità of her collection.
They're grateful to him. He has made their trip.

He almost falls out of the cockpit when he realizes that they've let go of his legs. That he's been balancing on his well-rounded stomach on the edge of the plane all this time.
He starts flailing, trying to clutch at either of them. & would have pulled them down with him into the streets of IV-century Rome if a jolt had not sent all 3 of them flying back inside, as the plane barely misses impaling itself on Trajan's column.
They lie sprawled on their backs like overturned garden pests, each twin apologizing to the other & blaming him for what almost happened.

They accuse him of trapping them in his private lives.

They lecture him on the difference between useful & harmful selfishness.

They draft a bill for an international agreement on worldwide enforcement of the death penalty for hi-jackers. Whose execution in an electric pilot seat they propose, in the 5 official working languages of the United Nations. Which both twins speak, read & write. & in all 5 of which they start jabbering while the plane dips. & bops. & zigzags.

He scrambles to his feet & into the pilot seat. Which has as yet not been juiced for executions.

They scramble after him. Still jabbering & lecturing & blaming, they hang over his shoulders. Criticizing every move he makes, every switch he pulls. Telling him that he doesn't know how to hold a straight eastern course. That he is losing the speed they've painstakingly built up over close to 17 centuries. Disagreeing with each other about which switch he should or should not pull next. Behaving in every way like parents who are jointly assisting their son with his homework.

They've made him so nervous, he has flown them into a snow storm. He can't see where they are, or where they're going.

Perhaps they're standing still, hovering over the same spot like a humming bird.

Perhaps they're circling over Eboracum (York) NE Britain, shortly after Belfortis Hamus Verus' Judean soldier began praying to the Christian God for the survival & subsequent victory of his Roman oppressors.

At last he'll get a chance to see his true predecessors. The men who really led his former lives, now that he has taken over. & is in full command of the plane. They can jabber all they like.

Because he is obviously the reincarnation of Belfortis

Hamus Verus, not of Belfortis Hamus. Not of the gouty father, but of the genius son. Who had also had a sap for a father.

Of William Blake rather than of a left-handed 17th-century-English printer & levelling ladies' man by the unknown name of Beaufort Hookker.

Into whose unhistorical life in York (Eboracum) NE England the twins flew him only to tease him, with their peculiar sense of humor.

To show him who he might have been, if he had been less gifted than he is. He is after all sufficiently acquainted with the known life of William Blake. He is after all a prof. of Eng. Lit.

Having been a genius for 2 lives in a row   (with a consistent posthumously computed I.Q. of 211; 1 point more than J. W. Goethe)   has exhausted his vital energies. Which he has therefore had to replenish for the first 45 years of his current existence. Gathering the strength for his imminent breakthrough as a great anthropological decoder/archeologist/architect . . . historian . . ./musician/painter/political figure . . . Writer. Or whatever else, in alphabetical order.

A combination of all the above. He is the first recognized universal genius since Emanuel Swedenborg. Whom he used to admire when he used to be William Blake.

Blake was 15 when Swedenborg died.

& has probably become another genius since then. William James. Jesse James. William S. Porter-O. Henry James Joyce. Einstein. Gertrude Stein. Rudolf Steiner. Sneaky-Pete Kaminstein.

Whereas he is descended from a straight line of mediocrities. Who get more mediocre as the line grows longer.

Who are occasionally   tantalizingly   the father/brother/ husband of a genius.

Who are bound together by an umbilical cord of careless wishes.

For an average daughter . . . fulfilled 7 times over . . .

For the easier life of a woman . . .

A crippled little girl's wish for reunion with her dead fairystory-telling mother: His inescapable rusty-haired freckle-faced recently recognized Irish concert-harpy wife. Maureen.

Who has trailed him all the way to fourth-century NE Britain . . .

He must keep flying   like the Dutchman   if he wants to be free of her. Faster & faster   deeper & deeper into his past. Until he reaches the first bodily manifestation of his soul.
   (Or whatever one calls the continued entity within a succession of bodies.)   When he still had a choice. Before he made the first careless wish that brought her into his life.

That led down the road of mediocrity & doomed all his subsequent incarnations to anonymity. & ineffectiveness. The way Cassandra was made ineffective when Apollo spat into her mouth when she spurned him. He must go back to that first time, at the outset of his being, when he spurned the life force & then played coy with it.

He sees nothing & no one. Not even the twins. The snow is falling too thickly. He has never seen snow fall so thickly. The flakes are enormous. Almost the size of his hand. & heavily perfumed.

They're camelias, not snow flakes.

& they're being showered upon a voluptuous honey-colored human body of indefinable age & indefinable sex male as well as female   that is reclining in a hammock of braided lianas. Which 8 honey-colored children   4 boys & 4 girls   are gently cradling at either end.

16 more children   8 girls & 8 boys   are perched in the branches overhead like honey-colored birds, dropping the camelia blossoms into the hammock.

& on the heads of a line of honey-colored adults alternatingly: 1 man   1 woman   1 man   1 woman   who are approaching at a respectful pace.

They're clad in short hair skirts, made of the wearer's own silky hair. Which has been thinly braided, & dyed. A deep purple for the women, a bright yellow for the men.

Each man carries a halved over-ripe purple fruit   the size of a water melon, but extremely mushy   on outstretched palms.

Each woman holds a bright yellow stalk of something that is probably some kind of cereal, only thicker   (about the thickness of a policeman's billy)   high above her head.

As each man or woman steps up to the hammock, 2 hands reach out.

They have been painted & decorated.

The left hand   which has been painted purple   wears long bright-yellow claws   (or perhaps birds' beaks)   at the finger tips, & a bracelet of bright-yellow feathers around the wrist.

The right hand is bright yellow, with purple claws   (or birds' beaks)   & purple feathers at the wrist.

Each man or woman bows.

The left hand parts the hair skirt in the front, while the right hand   according to sex   either impales the fruit or inserts the stalk.

If the fruit fails to be properly impaled, a tongue clicks loudly from within the hammock. Giving the signal for an all-around rhythmic clicking of tongues.   (With one exception.)

The crestfallen bearer returns to the end of the line. The woman behind him steps up.

If the same man blows his second chance, the 2 hands take the fruit from him, ceremoniously drop it to the ground with a splashy thud, & offer a yellow stalk, at the top of which 2 small bells   1 purple & 1 yellow   have been fastened with purple & yellow hair.

Once more the bearer returns to the end of the line, to a rhythmic clicking of tongues. The little bells tinkle derisively as he carries the stalk high above his head.

At his third turn, the bell-stalk is inserted into his rear, while the others click tongues & the children giggle. & chuck the bells as he passes near them.

After each adult has been attended to, the line forms a circle around the hammock.

The 2 hands begin to perform a slow seduction dance. Which culminates in a clapping together of the palms.

A round face, painted half purple/half yellow, framed by loose long half yellow/half purple hair, rises from the hammock with the slowness of the morning sun, & beams upon the circle.

Which breaks into a dance. Somewhat awkwardly, because of fruit & stalks which must be maintained in place if the bearer is to have a happy fruitful year ahead.

Which becomes increasingly difficult as the palms clap faster & faster. Faster & faster. Faster & faster.

Eventually nearly everyone trips & falls. Careful to fall on his or her back. Except for the men with the bell-stalks, who carefully fall on their faces.

He looks around for the twins. To see their reaction. What do they think of him now! As a Happy Hermaphrodite who is being worshipped as a symbol of fertility. A high priest of prosperity. A god who holds fulfillment in his painted claws. Or birds' beaks.

But the twins have disappeared. Fused within him as parents fuse in a child. Now he is both of them in one.

Unless they dived from the cockpit, in envious dismay.
He's on his own. & has never felt so powerful. Or so benign.

It takes him a full minute to realize that someone has been knocking at the door. With loud persistence.
& another 30 seconds to realize where he is. In a hotel room.
He assumes that he has had some kind of revelation. Which is too unprecedented an experience in his life to know what to do. He doesn't want any future Mr.-Mrs.-Miss-Ms Hookker/Hamus/Hermaphrodite to suffer mediocrities because of any careless spontaneity on his part. Because of the mechanical reply: "Enter!" to a knock on the door.

Which has opened.

It opens into the room. Forming a triangle with the shabby wall.
Mechanically he reads the number. 401. It has been painted over several times. He can see dirty white under dirty rust-red under dirty green. Under the flaking black.
His recently recognized c.-h. wife Maureen is standing on the threshold, disguised as a freckle-faced Irish chambermaid.
Her rust-red hair has been tucked untidily into a crest of white starch. Her feather duster is a disguised whip with a built-in electrical device which runs on a battery. With which over-ambitious jockeys shock-whip horses that run races under assumed names. & pass themselves off as thoroughbreds. & are either electrified into winning, or else collide in the bends with other horses. True thoroughbreds, that break their legs in the collision.
"Room service," she says with a freckled smirk.

Instead of the ingratiating smile to which he feels entitled, as a hotel guest.

A smile is part of the American way of life: he tells her: Recommended by the American Passport Office in its information sheet for passport applicants. "The Pp. Office welcomes photographs which depict the applicant as a relaxed & *smiling* person." A relaxed American face, smiling the American-way-of-life at scowling foreign border officials. Making them stop & think . . .

Her elaborate disguise is incomplete without the service-smile.

She shrugs. She didn't come here to be photographed.

Besides, she has a blue tooth on one side of her mouth which shows when she smiles. She's been wanting to get it capped, but she's scared. Of the pain more than of the money.

She has obviously come to kill him. Without his father's permission. Which she didn't bother to ask. She didn't go to Pennsylvania. Why should she? She has better things to do than help him fulfill himself.

What makes him think that he needs her help? He's been doing a first-rate job, killing himself, all these married years. Stifling whatever spark of talent he may have had inside him, for the sake of a youthful seducer's image. Of mod Mad. Ave. rather than strabismal Academe.

She sees no reason to meddle. & play midwife to his death. She no longer cares whether he lives or dies. He is free. From whatever love she once felt for him. As free as a bird.

'A dead duck & a cooked goose are also birds,' he says slowly. Still half in a daze.

What has she come for then? What does she want from him?

She wants him to get up. So that she can clean the room: she says tartly.

Why doesn't he go to the bathroom down the hall, & take a

shower, while she makes the bed. It's way past 11. High time to get up.

He stretches his legs. Which feel stiff from sitting cross-legged on the pillow he doesn't know for how long. & walks over to the window. The place through which light enlightenment enters a room.
Sparingly. The glass is filthy. Don't they ever wash their windows, in this hotel?
His disguised wife comes over & stands beside him.
For quite some time now she has been affianced to one of the 5 yellow-helmeted men down below who have been drilling the sidewalk outside the hotel entrance since the blueing hours of dawn.
They have stopped drilling. & are squatting/leaning/sitting on the fire hydrant, eating their lunch.
His wife's fiancé is the stocky one on the right. The one who is sitting on the hydrant, biting into a chicken leg.
She raps at the dirty glass until he looks up & sees her. He smiles. She waves to him. He waves the chicken leg.
She knows he'll be a faithful husband to her. One that doesn't run around in search of dopey-dupe fulfillment. He finds fulfillment in his job. He enjoys the therapy of working with his hands.
Which is more fulfilling than working with half a mind, & fretting with the other half about unrequited ambitions. She should have known better than to get herself hooked up with an incurable adolescent. A self-dissatisfied intellectual with a variety of better-than-average aptitudes. An amateur in everything but bed.
Her stocky yellow-helmeted fiancé has real talent. He has a beautiful singing voice. A beautiful basso profundo. He likes to sing while he works. & he's been singing with her when she plays her harp. They're thinking of going on consort tours, after they marry.
The man is singing now. *'Yo soy un hombre sincero . . .*

one of her favorite songs. She can't wait to be married to him.

'Marriage is so unhip,' he says. 'An outmoded paternalistic pig institution.'

Obviously she has learned nothing from past experience. & must be taught a lesson. If she's so talented she doesn't need a husband to support her.

'Don't bother teaching people lessons, unless you get paid for it,' she says tartly.

She needn't worry. He intends to get paid. Teaching is after all his one salaried profession.

He has managed to wrestle the feather duster from her idly hanging hand. & is whipping her with it. Forcing her to back up toward the bed. On which she falls   shocked; on her back looking up at him with round-eyed apprehension.

He rapes her. Rapidly. Perfunctorily. Trying not to see the freckles on her knee caps. Which might make him sentimental.

What will her faithful fiancé think of her now!

She is as limp as a rag doll when he pulls her up. By her starched white crest. & drags her to the window.

He opens the window & throws her out.

She floats down, still limp, her devious chambermaid's skirt billowing about her freckled knees like a parachute. Her hair is trailing behind her like a rust-red flag.

The 5 yellow-helmeted men have dropped their lunches the chicken leg   & are running with a yellow tarpaulin. Swishing it this way & that, under the window, like bullfighters their capes.

The stocky one   his wife's fiancé   tries to catch her in his arms. But she floats past him. She's always been elusive. Persistent, but elusive. That'll teach him to be faithful.

The man doffs his yellow helmet & yells his thanks up to the window.

Which is broken, he notices. She must have broken it with her chambermaid's heels. With which she had kicked when he threw her out.

'Happy birthday!' yells the man.

His wife must have told her fiancé that today is his birthday. Although she herself hadn't bothered to congratulate him.

He calls his thanks down in return. He's much obliged to be rid of her. Now he can go home again.

It is the thought of his 2 dead cats swaying from the radiator pipes in the empty apartment that makes him hesitate. Rather than the entrance of 2 policemen. Who have poured into his room with drawn guns. & look disconcertingly alike. & Irish. Like a middle-aging pair of Irish twins.

They're helping him into his pants. Clumsily, with their free right hands, since they're both left-handed, & won't put down their guns.

They, too, are wishing him a happy birthday as they dance clumsily around him, in their heavy boots.

As an afterthought, he changes the 2 dead swaying cat bodies into 2 hanged swaying plush cats. In case his third-person/second-sex autobiography becomes a bestseller. & is made into an underground movie.

The recently rich-&-recognized Irish concert-harpist had them custom-made by F. A. O. Schwarz, to look disconcertingly like Leon Katz & Catherine.

Whom she has hanged in effigy, to shock him into a

spiritual awakening, before she took off for the nunnery.
For an ashram in San Francisco. Where it is not yet 5 to noon. Where it is 5 to 9 a.m.
She is endowing the ashram with a house for cats. A luxurious pavilion with live-in veterinarians, as a tax deduction. To encourage young aspirants in the art of meditation by observing the smiling relaxation of cats.

Of their 2 live beloved cats. Which she has taken with her, in her private plane.
He doesn't want to cause the death of animals, even if that were to be the price of his success. The condition of his autobiography being made into a film. He loves & respects all forms of life. Even people.

Even women.
He has sincerely loved all the women to whom he has made love.

>   Yo soy un hombre sincero
>   Je suis une ombre sincère
>   I am a shadow of a truth.

The deafening applause of the noon siren greets him as he steps outside for the curtain call.
It is joined by another siren in the distance. Which draws closer. & shouts 'Bravo!' as it stops.
The 2 policemen step aside, making way for 5 or 6 white-tuxedoed gentlemen who have alighted from their powerful white limousine & come running toward him across the quaking plank that is still bridging the sidewalk. They cluster around him, asking for his autograph.

FICTION COLLECTIVE

books in print:

Reruns by Jonathan Baumbach
Museum by B. H. Friedman
Twiddledum Twaddledum by Peter Spielberg
Searching for Survivors by Russell Banks
The Secret Table by Mark Mirsky
98.6 by Ronald Sukenick
The Second Story Man by Mimi Albert
Things In Place by Jerry Bumpus
Reflex and Bone Structure by Clarence Major
Take It or Leave It by Raymond Federman
The Talking Room by Marianne Hauser
The Comatose Kids by Seymour Simckes
Althea by J. M. Alonso
Babble by Jonathan Baumbach
Temporary Sanity by Thomas Glynn
ϕ Null Set by George Chambers
Amateur People by Andrée Connors
Moving Parts by Steve Katz
Find Him! by Elaine Kraf
The Broad Back of the Angel by Leon Rooke
The Hermetic Whore by Peter Spielberg
Encores for a Dilettante by Ursule Molinaro
Fat People by Carol Sturm Smith
Meningitis by Yuriy Tarnawsky
Statements 1, an anthology of new fiction (1975)
Statements 2, an anthology of new fiction (1977)

available at bookstores
or from
GEORGE BRAZILLER, INC.